Time

Part Two: The Binding

Nicole Targaryen

Copyright © 2020 Nicole T.

This is a work of fiction. Names, characters, places, and incidents either are the product of the author's imagination or are used fictitiously, and any resemblance to actual persons, living or dead, events, or locales is entirely coincidental.

ISBN: 979-8-9855195-2-5

ISBN: 979-8-9855195-3-2

Front cover image by Nicole Targaryen

Book design by Nicole Targaryen

www.officialnicoletargaryen.wordpress.com

Acknowledgements

Once more, I'd like to thank God for providing me with the resources to write this book. I'd also like to express my gratitude to my family again for their unwavering support. Finally, I want to thank my muse, who inspired this series.

Table of Contents

Chapter Seventeen: The Game

Chapter Eighteen: The Enigma

Chapter Nineteen: The Senatorial Ball

Chapter Twenty: The Rift

Chapter Twenty-One: The Repair

Chapter Twenty-Two: The Division

Chapter Twenty-Three: The Agreements

Chapter Twenty-Four: The Decisions

Chapter Twenty-Five: The Conflict of Interest

Chapter Seventeen: The Game

"Put me down, put me down!" I shouted, pushing Lorne off me.

"What's wrong?" He asked.

"You…the Commander just saw you carrying me into my rooms!" I yelled, "and you said not to tell anyone!"

With those last words of scolding, my knees gave out beneath me. Thankfully, Lorne noticed and caught me before I could hit the ground. Even though I protested vehemently, he carried me straight to my bed and set me down.

"What do you need?" He tucked a piece of hair behind my ear.

"Water." I reached for the water bottle on my nightstand.

Lorne grabbed it and handed it to me. He watched me closely as I took a gulp of water. After I was satisfied, he set it back onto my nightstand and placed one of his hands on my forehead.

"You're kind of hot," he noted, "I should call a doctor."

"No!" I objected.

"You need medical attention, Azalyn." He said.

"Call Joyriak, she'll take care of me." I commanded.

"Azalyn…" he began.

"Just call her, please," I pleaded, "I'll see you at dinner."

He nodded reluctantly and turned to exit my rooms; he glanced back once more at the doorway before leaving. I sighed heavily and sunk into the fluffy pillows on my bed. Even though I was worried that I was having a very bad reaction to the shots, I wanted nothing more than to go to sleep.

"Aza?" Joyriak called, barely five minutes after Lorne had left. I propped myself up in bed as she entered.

"You look terrible!" She exclaimed, "what's wrong?"

"The... the stupid shots." I mumbled.

"Man, you're getting the worst of it, aren't you?" She chuckled lightly.

"Is this normal?" I croaked.

"Not normal…but it's not anything bad," she assured me, "some people have super bad reactions like you."

"So, I'm not dying?" I stuttered.

"No, you're not dying, Aza." She laughed.

"How much time do I have before dinner?" I asked weakly.

"About an hour…you're not going, though." She said.

"I have to…the Supreme Order Dignitaries are back." I pushed myself into a sitting position.

"Okay, well, take a nap," she ordered, "and I'll wake you up when it's time to get ready."

She helped me lay down.

"Thank you." I breathed as I closed my eyes.

I was woken from my nap by Joyriak feeling rejuvenated. The worst part of my reaction, it seemed, was over. Joyriak gently helped me prepare for dinner, constantly asking if I was okay to go. I assured her that I did, in fact, feel fine, and I could handle dinner. Actually, I was more than ready to get to dinner; my body had overcome its obstacle and had an abundance of energy to use.

As Joyriak prepared me for dinner, I resolved that I was going to use Lorne's slip-up to my advantage. Keylan would most likely be bothered by the implication of what he'd seen, so why shouldn't I mess with him just a bit? If nothing else, it would be a good way to teach him not to make assumptions and act jealous.

"Hey," I said to Joyriak, "these shots are crazy, huh?"

"Yeah," Joyriak chuckled, "they're a lot and they're really intense... they basically alter your body to be able to respond to the northern climate and diseases that you've never even been exposed to."

"That's one downside of serving Soturna," I sighed, "I barely had time to travel before, and for the past 10 years I've been locked in here."

"You got to go with the Commander to an island, though." She said.

"Yeah," I shrugged, "but it's uninhabited... I didn't even need to get shots or medication or anything.... it was completely cleaned out by the Supreme Order."

"It's kind of sad Leader Syphex did that." Joyriak muttered.

"What?" I frowned.

"Never mind," she smiled, "Leader Syphex is a great man who has brought our nation to prosperity."

I smiled in response, although I was quite suspicious of what I'd heard.

"Well, I'm off to dinner." I said as she finished readying me.

"Are you completely sure that you're okay?" She questioned.

"Yeah," I chirped, "I'll see you later!"

With that, I jogged out of my room and down the hall towards the banquet hall; I had to keep myself from skipping as I got closer. Keylan was back sooner than I thought he would be, which made me happy, and my fight with the northern travel shots had left me feeling energetic.

"Azalyn!" Lorne beamed as I entered the banquet hall.

"Hello, Lorne." I grinned.

He leaned in close to me as he offered his arm. I took his arm and allowed him to lead me to my chair.

"Are you feeling better?" He whispered.

I nodded cheerfully and sat in my place. Lorne took his place beside me and studied me carefully, trying to see if I was lying.

"I'm okay." I assured him, placing my hand on his knee comfortingly.

A blush arose in Lorne's cheeks, and he smiled. He took my hand and intertwined his fingers with mine.

"I'm glad you are," he responded, "I was worried about you."

"Joyriak takes good care of me." I told him.

He smiled at me as everyone else took their seats. I could feel Keylan's eyes on me, even though they were currently veiled by his helmet. With a quick glance in his direction, I noticed that General Armande was also watching Lorne and I with a curious expression. I cleared my throat and positioned my body so that I was facing towards the table instead of towards Lorne, dropping his hand as I did so.

"How was the mission?" My father inquired.

"Everything went quite well, thank you." Captain Plutan responded.

"So, there is nothing…. nothing bad to report?" Senator Varros inquired.

"Not at all." Hanew quipped.

"I'd like to inquire after your trip as well," I spoke up, "but I'm afraid I'm ill-informed on it."

"I'm in the same boat as you, Aza." Lorne chuckled.

I turned and offered him a warm smile, which he returned gleefully.

"Did anything interesting happen while we were gone?" Hanew changed the subject.

"I'm afraid not, General." I replied curtly.

"Commander, did you want to take off your helmet?" My mother questioned Keylan.

I directed my attention back to him, waiting to see if he would storm out again. Waves of relief washed over me when I saw him lift the helmet off his head and set it neatly beside his chair as Captain Plutan had done. My eyes trailed over his face, pausing as I looked at his lips. Unfortunately for me and my sudden spark of playfulness, he looked unbothered by how friendly Lorne and I were being.

"Lorne, I have to apologize for not finishing your tour of the castle." I turned to him, speaking in hushed tones.

"It's all right, we'll do it another time." He grinned.

"If we have time." I laughed.

The chalis set the first course in front of us and I shakily picked up my fork. I wondered why I was so jittery since I felt fine now. As I lifted the fork to my mouth, I dropped it onto the floor, and blushed in embarrassment. I glanced over at a chali, who nodded and went to retrieve another fork for me.

"You're not completely better yet, are you?" Lorne whispered.

I shook my head and sighed, not wanting to explain that I did feel better, I was just shaky for some reason. I hoped that I wasn't nervous or scared as I feared I was, because that would mean I was losing my grip on Keylan.

"Here, just use mine for now." Lorne handed me his fork.

"Lorne, it's okay…Aisha just went to get me one." I pushed his hand away.

"You need to eat." He argued.

"Lorne, it'll only take her a couple seconds." I said.

Aisha handed me the fork as I finished my sentence.

"See?" I smirked.

He rolled his eyes and shook his head jokingly, making me giggle.

"Convenient." He scoffed.

"I know, right?" I laughed.

"You two seem to be getting along better." Hanew interrupted.

"Yeah…Lorne's been very…helpful lately." I beamed.

"Anything for the most beautiful Cerulea in the world." Lorne winked.

"I'm the only *Cerulea* in the world, Lorne," I chucked, "other than Miransi, of course, who is still too young to be considered a beauty by the likes of you."

"Most beautiful princess then." He said.

"Well..." I began.

"Oh, just take the compliment." He scoffed.

I shrugged and turned back to my food, trying to hide my smile. A glass shattered and we both turned our attention towards the sound to see pieces of Keylan's glass littered across the table. Keylan grabbed his helmet, pushed away from the table, and stood, looming over all of us.

"Have someone bring my dinner to my room." He commanded.

He marched out of the room, the heavy wooden doors slamming behind him. The Senator, Senatress, and Lorne all looked traumatized; I was reminded that they had never seen one of the Commander's infamous outbursts before. I was sure I looked the same the first time Keylan had acted that way in front of me.

"I'm sorry, Commander Rixar is very stressed from the mission," Captain Plutan apologized, "he had us finish it in double time and I think it took a toll on him."

My eyes widened at Captain Plutan's statement. The memory of Keylan promising me he would be back as soon as possible came flooding back. If he had done this all for me, and I had repaid him by playfully flirting with Lorne, then I would feel awful.

"I'll bring it to him." I offered.

"Cerulea, you don't have to do that." Hanew returned.

"I'm actually feeling ill anyways," I excused myself, "I can bring the Commander his dinner on my way to my rooms."

"You shouldn't do that if you're ill," Lorne argued, "I'll do it for you."

"No, I'm fine, thank you." I smiled before rushing off to the kitchens.

I knew everyone was going to keep arguing with me if I stayed a moment longer; why the General and Lorne seemed so opposed to me bringing Keylan his dinner was a mystery to me. It was apparent that everyone at that table thought Lorne and I were romantically involved, even Lorne; there was no way any of them were suspicious of Keylan and me.

As I waited for Keylan's food to be ready, thoughts began to race in my mind. I had tried to keep the playful flirting to a minimum, both for Keylan and for Joyriak, but what if I had taken it too far? What if I had ended up ruining my relationship with Keylan instead of teasing him?

"Here you go, Cerulea." Shamasi smiled as he handed me the tray.

"Thanks." I grinned.

I hurried out the back door to Keylan's rooms. My officer, who had previously followed me into the kitchen, struggled to keep up. I considered handing her the tray and just running to Keylan's rooms; it wasn't like she didn't know where to go. I pushed the thought down as I saw a couple chalis cleaning the corridors on my way to his rooms.

"I have the Commander's dinner." I informed the officers when they did not immediately open the doors for me.

I frowned as I watched them share a look through their helmets. One of them nodded, emitting a mechanical-sounded sigh as they did so. The other pressed their wristband to the lock, making the doors slide open. I furrowed my brows at this; had Keylan really locked the doors behind him? Had he really locked the doors on *me*?

"Return to my rooms." I told my officer as I slipped inside.

The doors slid shut behind me with a loud noise, causing me to flinch. I noticed, with some annoyance, that all the lights were off. I stumbled over to the coffee table, banging my knees against it in the process, and set the tray of food down. I then padded further into the room, searching for Keylan in the darkness.

I nearly screamed when I felt two strong arms wrap around me from behind. One was wrapped around my waist, holding me in place, while the other one hooked underneath my chin, almost choking me and keeping me from speaking. I struggled for a moment, when I heard Keylan's voice.

"I leave for less than three days, and you run off with *him?*" Keylan's deep voice hissed.

I tried to speak but was prevented from doing so by Keylan's hand.

"I finished my mission in double time…all for you," he continued, "and you repay me by being with *him?*"

I sensed his grip loosen with the last word and seized the opportunity to turn around and face him. He dropped both his arms as I turned, then raised them to pull me to him. I could tell that he either had more to say to me, or he wasn't going to let me leave without me offering an explanation for my actions.

I truly wanted to offer an explanation, but I couldn't find the words. Now that he had confirmed my fears, I *really* didn't want to tell him that it was all a stupid game. I also didn't want to tell him that all of this had started because I had gotten the northern travel shots so I could go to the base him. Instead of speaking, I reached up to gently kiss him. As I'd predicted, he quickly pushed me away.

"That's not going to work." He scolded.

"I'm sorry." I apologized.

"Are you going to tell me what the hell is going on?" He asked.

"I went to the doctor and got…" I looked up at him.

He squinted his eyes at me, and I guessed what he was thinking. I was slightly offended that he thought I was such a slatternly person but decided to continue anyways.

"I got some shots," I continued, "and while I was giving Lorne a tour of the castle, I got sick, and he took me back to my rooms."

"So, *why* would he ask me not to tell anyone about the incident?" he pressed.

"I didn't want anyone knowing I was sick." I said.

He scoffed and pushed away from me, obviously thinking that I was lying. He walked away from me and turned on the lights, alerting me that I was about to be thrown out of his rooms.

"I got the northern travel shots!" I blurted out.

He froze in place.

"You…you what?" He stammered, still turned away from me.

"I went to the doctor," I said, "and I got the northern travel shots."

He stiffened.

"Why would you do that?" He growled.

"I…I wanted to…" I stuttered.

"You wanted to what?" He turned and stormed towards me, "to run off with the Senatorial Son? To be the wife of some *boy*, to be a Senatress instead of fulfilling your duties as the Cerulea of Asphoamist?"

"No, you moron!" I shouted, "I want to go with you! I want to be with *you*."

A confused expression washed over his face. He froze once more, looking as if he were thinking much too hard about what I'd just said.

"When you go back to the Supreme Order Base," I said, "I want to go with you. I'll stay there with you until it's time for me to come home and prepare to be Lumina."

He blinked in confusion.

"I want to marry you, Keylan." I told him.

"You're not ready to get married yet, Aza." He breathed as if in disbelief.

"Maybe not," I shrugged, "but neither of us know how all of this is going to end, and if something happens and they try to split us up... well, we'll have an excuse to stay together."

I smiled brightly up at him, hoping he would receive my words well.

"Are you still sick?" he suddenly inquired.

I frowned, hoping he wasn't trying to avoid the subject.

"I feel a lot better now." I replied.

He nodded and then looked down at the floor. I stepped towards him and placed a hand on his cheek.

"You got those shots so that you could come home with me," he said, "so that we could get married, and no one could tear us apart."

"I hated being away from you." I admitted.

"I know what you mean." He chuckled.

He still seemed to be a bit awestruck by the situation, so I decided I would let him be for now.

"Let's go lay down and watch a holoprogram," I suggested, "we'll talk more in the morning."

Keylan followed me to his bedroom, but he seemed as if he had more to say. Even so, we settled onto the bed, and I began flipping through channels on the holoprojector. Next to me, Keylan shifted uncomfortably and stared at the projection before us with furrowed brows.

"Are you okay?" I asked.

"Yes... I'm just... I guess I'm just surprised," he confessed, "that you would do something like that for me."

"Of course, I would," I smiled, "but, I mean, you *did* finish your mission quicker so you could return to me, so I guess we're even."

He still seemed somewhat bothered.

"Did you not want me to get the shots?" I inquired, "do you not want me to come back with you?"

"I didn't want you to get the shots." He replied.

"Oh." I mumbled.

I felt like I had been punched in the gut. I had just gone through hours of inconvenient symptoms so I could be with him forever, and now he was telling me that he didn't want the same things I did.

"I didn't mean..." he stammered, "I just...you didn't have to do that for me."

I stared at him, waiting for him to continue.

"You should have waited for me, so I could help you," he breathed, "I feel so bad that you went through all that without me."

"It's okay, Keylan," I smiled, "I wanted to do it."

"I don't like that Lorne was the one helping you." He added.

"Oh." I chuckled.

I finally realized why he was upset. He wasn't mad that I'd gotten the northern travel shots, nor did he dislike my plans. He was upset that I had done it while he was gone and that Lorne was the one to help me, instead of him.

"You are mine," he continued, "aren't you?"

"I am yours and you are mine." I whispered.

"I love you so much." He said.

"I love you." I smiled.

Keylan took my hand and kissed the top of it as Lorne had done so many times before. Keylan's kiss felt different; it was softer, yet more confident.

"Now, what are we going to watch?" He asked as he lounged into the pillows; his arm outstretched towards me.

I snuggled underneath his arm, getting comfortable against his body.

"I Love Lucy!" I exclaimed, flipping to the Historical Films Channel.

"That show is over a thousand years old," Keylan groaned, "it'll be so grainy we'll barely be able to see what's going on."

"It's still funny," I argued, "just as funny as it was in the 1900s."

"Fine." Keylan sighed.

Although I was excited to watch the show, I soon fell asleep. I would awake every so often as a laugh rumbled through Keylan's chest and I'd smile at the fact that he was enjoying the show he had protested.

"Hey, hey!" Keylan shook me awake.

"No!" I protested sleepily.

"I will literally carry you back to your rooms if you don't get up."
He threatened.

"We'll get caught." I mumbled sleepily, rubbing my eyes.

"You and Lorne didn't get caught." He snapped.

"Ugh, really?" I rolled my eyes and stood up.

Keylan watched me as I slipped my shoes back on and straightened up my dress. He followed me as I slipped through the castle corridors, trying to get back to my rooms quickly. I realized as I walked that I felt very well-rested. I had gone to bed at a reasonable time the night before and would probably not need any more sleep now. If there was one positive to the northern travel shots' side effects, it was me going to sleep and rising earlier than normal.

"Come on." I pulled Keylan's hand as we reached the door to my rooms.

He gave me a questioning look.

"Officer 731," I commanded, "tell my halcyns that I woke up early and invited Key- Commander Rixar to my rooms so that he could tell me about his mission."

The officer, my personal guard for the next 15 minutes, bowed in response. I looked to the two officers guarding my rooms.

"Officers 927 and 284, you will say the same." I demanded.

They both bowed in response.

"You're going to lie?" Keylan raised an eyebrow, "I thought you were totally against lying no matter what the reason... and you know, if I would have known you were going to do this, we could have just stayed...."

I cleared my throat to interrupt him.

"Commander Keylan Rixar of the Supreme Order," I said in a mockingly proper voice, "I, Cerula Azalyn Naiya Windskae of the Asphoamist Kingdom, invite you into my rooms to tell me about your mission because I woke up earlier than normal."

"I accept the invitation." He smirked, strolling into my room.

Keylan sat down on one of the couches in my sitting room, making himself comfortable.

"Commander," I jested, "are you going to sit on *my* couch without *my* permission?"

"Cerulea," he returned, "are you going to command the Commander of the Supreme Order?"

I scrunched my nose at him, making him chuckle. He motioned for me to join him, and I obeyed, draping my legs across his and leaning back on the couch.

"So, are you going to tell me what this mission was about?" I queried.

"I don't want to scare you." He responded.

"I won't get scared!" I exclaimed.

"The Canadians have penetrated the border between us and them," he explained, "the Supreme Order base was attacked by a small army and there were plans to attack the kingdoms."

"Okay," I chuckled nervously, "now I'm a little nervous... not scared! Just nervous."

"I took care of them for you." He assured me, pulling me towards him.

I bit my lip as I thought over the situation; I hated the Canadian government and everything they had done to us. They were trying to break up the peaceful nation of Soturna and hurt everyone here. I wanted them wiped out once and for all, even though this thought went against my better judgement.

"I want to take over Canada." I stated.

He stared at me with surprise in his eyes.

"I want to be... I want to be the Lumina of Canada," I continued, "but it won't be Canada when I'm done... it will be part of Asphoamist... a part of *my* kingdom."

Visions of the war flashed through my mind. The memory of Keylan telling me about his past and how they had hurt his family burned brightly. I felt my heart quicken and my face go red as my anger continued to grow.

"Really?" Keylan asked.

"It's what I want more than anything, now," I told him, "I want to hurt them for hurting all of us... for hurting you and your family."

"Then, we'll do it…together," he reassured me, "if it's the last thing I do, I will make you the Lumina of Canada."

"And we'll take revenge on everyone who hurt your family," I added, "and you will be my Lumin."

I saw pain and sadness flash across his face as the memory returned to him.

"Hey," I said, effectively distracting him, "you still need to train me to use a lasersword."

"Tonight." He grinned.

"Do you promise?" I asked.

"I promise." He replied.

"Good." I said, snuggling into his chest.

I knew now that the threat of Canada was growing with each passing day. At the start of The Reforming, the Canadians had taken family and friends from me, as well as important members of Soturna's government. As if that wasn't enough, they had hurt or killed the only family Keylan had left, wounding him so deeply that he was prone to emotional outbursts and fits of jealousy. I vowed that I would make them pay for every single thing they did, for all the pain they had caused.

Keylan expertly avoided political topics in the rest of the conversations we had that morning because he knew I was getting upset. I wondered why he wasn't more upset; they had taken everything from him, shouldn't he be furious? Was I wrong for being angry?

We split as we heard a knock on the door. I slipped into a chair opposite and tried to straighten myself up.

"Come in." I said.

The doors slid open to reveal my alysseas and Joyriak. Their lack of astonishment at Keylan's presence told me they'd been informed he was here. I made a mental note to thank the officers who had covered for us. Although, it wasn't like they had a choice; Keylan would make sure they suffered if they disobeyed my orders, and they knew that.

"Hello, time to get ready already?" I said, putting on a show of formality for them.

"Yes, Cerulea." Joyriak replied, just as formally.

"Well, Commander," I rose to my feet and stretched my hand out towards him, "I thank you very much for telling me about the Supreme Order's mission."

"You're welcome, Cerulea." He shook my hand, his eyes boring into mine and sending me a secret message.

Keylan then strolled out of my rooms, drawing the eyes of both me and my companions. Joyriak turned her gaze back to me and I quickly peeled my eyes from his retreating form, although I could tell from her suspicious look that she knew something was up. Still, I was given no indication that morning that Joyriak or any of my other alysseas, who had apparently tagged along to see Keylan, were suspicious of Keylan and me.

I felt as if I were floating as I made my way to breakfast. I *really* liked having Keylan back and I wanted to see him as much as possible. I had missed his beautiful face, his deep voice, and his strong physique more than I would ever admit to anyone, including him.

"Good morning, Aza," Lorne greeted me, "you look much better."

"I am!" I chirped happily, "I slept very well last night."

Lorne continued to chat cheerfully with me through breakfast, gaining a less than friendly reaction from Keylan. He knew very well there was nothing between Lorne and me, but he still did not seem comfortable with us being friends; perhaps he was suspicious of Lorne. I had to admit, even I was still suspicious of Lorne and his intentions.

Lorne continued to chatter as we walked to the meeting room. In fact, every opportunity he had, he was talking to me. Even when my responses started to get shorter, he continued to chatter as if his life depended on it.

"Your highnesses," the Senator said as we broke for lunch, "I was wondering if we might have some private meetings."

"If everyone is all right with it," my father answered, "we can cancel this afternoon's meetings."

"That would be perfect," Hanew replied, "we're still getting settled back in after the mission."

"Wonderful," my mother smiled, "then we will see you all at dinner."

We all shuffled out of the meeting room, off to our respective lunch spaces. I shot a glance in Keylan's direction, wondering if maybe I could sneak off to see him after lunch. I thought it might be difficult, since Lorne seemed to be watching me like a hawk.

I was glad to have a break from Lorne during lunch. My parents were awfully quiet, making me wonder if something bad had happened; perhaps it had something to do with why the Senator and Senatress wanted to meet with them privately. What could they possibly be discussing that they wouldn't want me, Lorne, and the Supreme Order Dignitaries to know about?

After lunch, I hurried back to my rooms, afraid that Lorne might catch me. I liked spending time with him, but he seemed to be getting a bit too attached. Besides, I knew Keylan didn't particularly like me spending time with him and I understood his reservations. After all, Lorne, along with everyone else, was under the impression that I was single.

I decided after about an hour of solitude in my rooms that I should squeeze in a training session. Unfortunately for my physique, I'd barely been training recently since we had been so busy with meetings. I'd gotten a couple hours in here and there, enough to keep me in good shape, but not enough to build strength. If Keylan was going to teach me to use laserswords, I needed to be in *amazing* shape, especially since Keylan was rumored to be an *incredible* lasersword fighter.

About half an hour into my training session, my mother entered and called for me. I was peeved at the interruption but decided to go to her anyways. I knew that she wouldn't interrupt me if it wasn't important to do so.

"Yes, maima?" I responded.

"Why don't you get changed back into your dress and join me in the arena?" She smiled.

"Is something wrong?" I inquired.

"No," she beamed, "everything's perfectly fine."

With that, she turned on her heel and left the gym. I sighed and packed my gym bag before thanking my trainer and leaving. I really wanted a longer training session, but I had to keep my family and my royal duties first.

"What is it?" I queried as I joined her on the viewing deck above the arena.

She smiled and nodded her head towards the arena below us. In the center of the arena was Lorne, sparring with who I presumed to be one of his men-in-waiting. I watched with mild interest, noting his mistakes as well as his skill.

"You...do you want me to fight with him?" I stammered.

"No, just watch." She laughed.

"You…you want me to stand here and watch him fight someone?" I questioned.

"What do you think of him?" She asked.

"Of Lorne?" I clarified.

"Yes." She replied.

"He's all right, I guess," I sighed, "he's nice and funny sometimes, but a little too chatty for me."

I could tell that my mother was not pleased with my answer, but she did know I was brutally honest. If she didn't want to know my honest thoughts about him, she shouldn't have asked. She rested her hand atop mine in a comforting gesture.

"I think you should make an effort to get to know him better." She suggested.

"Why?" I frowned.

"It will be good for the alliance." She responded shortly.

We turned our attention back to Lorne and his opponent. As we did so, Lorne happened to look up at me. He gave me a smile before knocking his opponent of his feet. He lifted his sparring sword in the air triumphantly, showing off to the others who had gathered around the arena. I joined in their applause, watching Lorne beam with pride. With one more glance up at me, he stripped off the white shirt he was wearing and threw it to the side.

"He is quite handsome, is he not?" My mother smirked, "and fit as well, it would seem."

"Well, Joyriak thinks so." I scoffed.

"Is that why you're not interested?" She pressed.

"I wasn't interested before she told me she liked him." I shrugged.

"Hmm." She replied.

"Maima, can I have the gym for tonight?" I inquired, "after dinner?"

"Whatever for?" She returned.

"I need some training time," I answered, "it's really important that I'm in good shape should something else happen."

"I'll arrange it." She said.

"Thank you maima," I hugged her tightly, "I'll see you at dinner."

She smiled as I waltzed back to my rooms to prepare for dinner. I told the halcyns stationed outside to call for my sphoas, saying that I needed to freshen up before I went to dinner. They obeyed my commands and my sphoas were there soon after to clean me up and arrange my hair beautifully.

"Can I change my dress?" I queried.

"Is something wrong with this dress?" Lahani inquired.

"No, not at all," I assured her, "I just wanted to wear something a bit breezier tonight. It's very warm, you know."

I walked over to my closet, my sphoas trailing behind me.

"Like this." I held up a strapless, low-cut, metallic blue dress.

My sphoas shared a confused and anxious look, and I understood why. Their precious, innocent, little princess never wore anything so revealing. This particular dress was a gift from yet another visiting dignitary who incorrectly assumed that, because I was an adult, I would wear such a fashionable and revealing dress.

"Are you sure, Cerulea?" Erri questioned, "it might be uncomfortable."

"Yes, but it will keep me from being too hot." I returned.

They all nodded and set about getting me in the dress, which barely covered my chest and only stayed up because of the stiff fabric it was made of. The fabric was a beautiful, metallic blue infinity cloth, which made the dress look as if it were being held up by strings. It was adorned with scale-like ruffles and hugged my body perfectly; I knew it would be the perfect thing to wear to impress Keylan tonight.

I strutted into the dining hall and hid my smile as Lorne, Hanew, and Chasta's jaws dropped; their reactions made me feel like I was in a movie. I wondered if Plutan and Keylan were doing the same underneath their helmets. I was sure they were, since their heads seemed to follow me as I walked.

"Wow, Aza." Lorne breathed.

"Do you like it?" I chirped, "the Senator of Raeganar gave it to me."

"It's gorgeous, I love the fabric," Lorne reached out a hand towards my waist, "may I?"

I nodded, and he gently touched the fabric around my waist.

"Infinity cloth?" He inquired.

"Yep!" I responded.

"This is a pretty new invention, isn't it?" he marveled.

"It is!" I exclaimed, "it's a bit uncomfortable but still beautiful."

"Shall we?" Hanew interrupted, his voice seeming to catch in his throat.

I awkwardly shuffled to my seat, allowing Lorne to pull my chair out for me. It took all of my focus to sit down properly without crumpling the fabric or looking unnecessarily clumsy. I assumed I had done a good job of this, as both Chasta and Hanew still seemed enamored with me.

Captain Plutan removed her helmet, and I expected for Keylan to as well, but he did not. I wondered if I had unintentionally angered him in some way or if he was disgusted by my appearance. My cheeks flushed as my gaze drifted down to my lap where I was picking anxiously at the fabric of my dress.

"Hey," Lorne smiled and grabbed my hand, "don't worry, you look gorgeous."

"Thanks." I blushed.

Suddenly, Keylan pushed his chair back from the table, causing a loud screech to echo through the dining hall. Everyone's attention turned to him, their eyes wide. Keylan towered above the table, staring down at us for a moment, then stormed towards the door. Once he reached it, he turned back towards the table.

"I will be taking dinner in my rooms again," he announced loudly, "if the Cerulea's dress, which I assume is being worn to gloat over Asphoamist's connections, allows her to move properly, she may bring me my dinner."

The slamming of the doors behind him made me flinch as his words cut me. I wasn't sure if this was a clever ploy or not, but regardless, I felt a lump rising in my throat. I coughed to clear it, then raised my eyes to the Supreme Order Dignitaries across the table from me. I could feel that my anger was showing on my face.

"I apologize if the Supreme Order Dignitaries misunderstood my ensemble," I said, "and I apologize that Commander Rixar has so grossly misunderstood my intentions. Now, if you'll excuse me, I will bring the Commander his food and make my intentions clear in person."

I stood up from the table, and Lorne rose with me.

"I'm sorry, too," Lorne said to them, "I'm sorry that your Commander can't see in his stupid helmet... because if he could see, he would know that Azalyn looks beautiful and that she deserves compliments, not insults."

"Lorne!" his father scolded.

"No!" Lorne returned angrily, "Aza is one of the kindest people I've met, and I won't let people push her around because of that. She is my friend, and I am going to protect her."

Everyone at the table, including me, seemed very taken aback by Lorne's sudden and uncharacteristic outburst.

"So, *I* will bring the Commander his dinner," he said, "and I will tell him this myself."

"No, you won't," I hissed, "I appreciate you trying to help me Lorne, but you're angry and you're going to do something you'll regret. *I* will go, the Commander asked for *me*."

"Your excellencies," the Senator rambled nervously, "I would like to apologize for my son's disrespectful comments directed at the Commander."

The Senatress was too shocked to say anything, her face incredibly pale.

"It's perfectly fine," Hanew sighed, seeming incredibly calm, "he's a twat anyways."

I turned towards Hanew, my jaw slightly dropping in utter shock. Everyone's eyes widened as we looked at the General. The Lieutenant and Captain seemed rather unaffected, obviously used to these sorts of unprofessional comments from him; perhaps he made such comments in private with them often. I tried to compose myself as I wondered what their true feelings were towards Keylan.

"Well, um," I cleared my throat, "I'd better be off, then."

"You don't have to do this." My mother assured me.

"I'm perfectly capable." I returned.

She nodded, realizing I was determined to prove Keylan wrong. There was a hint of worry in my parents' eyes, as if they were afraid I would tell him off and he would hurt me. They were absolutely right to worry in the first respect; I was *definitely* going to tell him off.

I marched straight to Keylan's rooms as soon as I'd received his tray. I sent my personal officer back to my room, where she would stay until Keylan, or I, called for her. The officers stationed outside Keylan's rooms did not hesitate in opening the doors to his rooms, obviously sensing the anger radiating off of me.

"All right, jerk!" I shouted, prepared to begin my rant.

I slammed the tray down on the coffee table and Keylan turned from the window, jumping at the sound.

"You have ten seconds to grovel at my feet and apologize." I snapped, folding my arms over my chest.

He mirrored my movements

"Apologize?" he scoffed, "apologize for what?"

"Are you serious?" I scoffed.

"You should be apologizing to me." He argued.

My mouth dropped open again in surprise, but I quickly closed it as the anger built up inside of me. I shook my head slowly at him, letting him know I was seconds from absolutely exploding.

"You waltz in there wearing that *gorgeous* dress," he ranted, "and then you started flirting with that boy again, even though we *just* had a conversation about this!"

"He was asking me about the fabric, and I responded," I snapped, "how is that flirting?"

"You were holding his hand." He quipped.

"He took my hand because I was picking at the dress fabric," I yelled, "which *you* would know that I do when I'm nervous if you ever paid attention to me like he does!"

"You twist the fabric between your fingers." He disagreed.

I was taken aback at his response; he was correct of course, because I did *usually* twist the fabric of my clothing between my fingers. However, tonight I couldn't do that because the fabric was too tight on me.

"I watch you as often as I am able," he continued, "partially because I love you and partially because I want to be ready to protect you if something happens."

"I've told you before," I countered, "I'm perfectly capable of protecting myself, Keylan."

He stepped towards me and placed his hands on my waist.

"You can protect yourself wearing this?" he whispered.

"I... I don't know," I stammered, "perhaps."

He chuckled and pulled away from me, looking me over.

"I really am sorry if I made you feel bad," he apologized, "you do look gorgeous in it."

His eyes studied every inch of the dress carefully.

"If that stupid boy was more intelligent, though," he said, "he would have complimented *you* instead of the dress. You are the only reason that dress looks so beautiful."

"He did compliment me, later." I laughed.

"And how did he describe your radiance?" he joked.

"He said I was beautiful." I returned with a smile.

"Not good enough," he smirked, "I could think of better adjectives to describe you."

"Such as?" I giggled.

"Glorious, dazzling," he listed, "exquisite, stunning..."

"Oh, really?" I grinned.

He kissed me gently.

"Um, one more thing," I said, pulling away, "why did you insinuate that I was wearing this to brag about our connections with the other kingdoms? And why did you insinuate that I couldn't move in the dress?"

"Well, the latter I think is obvious," he answered, "I'm very upset about how tight that dress is... not only because I feel as though you can't properly move in it so as to defend yourself, but also because Armande and Chasta and that stupid boy were gawking at you."

"And the former insult?" I pressed.

"An experiment." He shrugged.

"An experiment?" I scoffed, "what is your obsession with doing crazy things as experiments?"

"Things have been moving slow lately," he said, "I wanted to gauge where everyone was at in relation to the alliance."

"And?" I pressed

"I... I don't want the other kingdoms getting too comfortable or thinking they're too powerful," he replied, "they need to know their place and remember that we are in charge."

"So, it's a power play?" I scoffed.

"No, I just..." he sighed, "listen, you know it's strange that the Senatorial Family asked to meet privately with your family yesterday... what if they want to unite and rise up against the Supreme Order?"

"They wouldn't do that," I said, "everyone loves the Supreme Order."

"Everyone?" he pressed.

My mind drifted back to Joyriak's whisper that morning.

"It's probably nothing," I shrugged, "maybe they think Lorne and I are dating or something... or will date or something."

He squinted at me.

"So, you admit that most people would think the two of you are dating?" he asked.

"I mean... we're friends and we're close in age," I said, "so... maybe."

"So, everyone thinks you wore that dress to impress *him*?" he spat.

"You know I wore it to impress you!" I exclaimed in exasperation, "why isn't that enough?"

His gaze floated back down to the metallic blue dress.

"Which is why you wore it to *dinner*?" he asked, "in front of *everyone*?"

"What, you think I'll waste my time putting this on for the one hour I'm with you before we go to sleep?" I scoffed.

"You could wear it overnight." He suggested.

"I... Keylan, this is ridiculously uncomfortable," I snorted, "I am *not* going to sleep in this."

"So, why wear it if it's uncomfortable?" he questioned.

"I just *told you*," I spat, "to impress *you*, dimwit!"

He hummed in response, then turned his attention to his tray on the coffee table. He frowned as he looked it over.

"Where's yours?" he inquired.

"I can't carry two trays Keylan," I rolled my eyes, "besides, do you want everyone to know I'm eating dinner with you?"

"I'm ordering your dinner to be brought here." He pushed past me.

"I got it!" I shouted, running past him and opening the doors.

Keylan's two officers turned to look at us.

"Inform my personal officer to tell the chalis I'll be having dinner privately," I ordered one of them, "and that she, the *officer*, is to bring me my tray here."

He bowed and went on his way. I closed the doors and turned back to Keylan.

"Go change." He suddenly ordered.

"What?" I frowned.

"Go change." He repeated.

"Why?" I crossed my arms over my chest.

"You can't do lasersword training in that." He motioned to the dress.

"Wait," I squealed excitedly, "you're really going to teach me tonight?!"

"I did promise," he said, "besides, I overheard that you'd reserved the gym for tonight.

"Yay!" I shouted, running to him.

I wrapped my arms tightly around his torso, squeezing him.

"You are the best!" I yelled.

"I know," he chuckled, "now go change."

"Okay!" I grinned.

I shuffled as quickly as possible out of the door and down the hallway, until I heard the thumping of boots quickly approaching me. I turned, only to see Keylan jogging towards me.

"You didn't take an officer with you?" he hissed angrily.

"I... there was only one left," I stammered, "I didn't want you to be unprotected."

"Me?" he exclaimed, "what about you? Walking all alone in *that*?"

"Um..." I frowned.

"You need to be protected," he said, "you can't walk to your rooms all alone. It's not safe right now."

"Well, then you accompany me." I returned.

"That's what I plan to do." He nodded quickly.

I rolled my eyes at him and continued on my way. He followed me into my rooms and was let in without hindrance by the officers stationed outside. I wondered if they would let any Supreme Order Dignitary in here, or just him. It made me wonder how private my rooms really were when they were guarding them.

"Do you need help getting out of that?" Keylan questioned.

"Um, I can call my sphoas." I sputtered.

"I'll do it." He offered.

"Okay." I mumbled nervously.

I turned around and allowed him to unlace the dress. His warm fingers brushed against my skin as he undid the laces carefully. I held the front of the dress to my chest, protecting my modesty as the dress came undone under his fingers. Once he was finished, I turned sheepishly and excused myself before running into my closet.

I closed the doors behind me and let the dress slip off me. I had no slip underneath this dress, as it was too tight to allow for one.

I shifted through my training and dance outfits, searching for the perfect thing to wear. I finally decided on a fashionable yet functional ensemble; the bottoms were tight leggings made of spandex which allowed for movement, while the top was looser and made of a combination of spandex and mesh fabric. The top did show a bit of my midriff, which I inspected carefully to ensure that I had not lost my muscle tone due to my lack of training. I pulled my hair out of its up-do, allowing it to fall down my back in a cascade of curls, then slicked it up into a ponytail. Finally, I pulled on some grey sneakers to complete my outfit. I looked myself over once more in the mirror, gave myself an encouraging smile, and strutted back out to Keylan.

To my elation, he seemed just as impressed as he had when I was wearing my dress. I didn't think I looked half as beautiful without the dress and fancy hair, but his reaction had boosted my confidence. Once I had grabbed my things, we strolled out of my rooms and back into his. My officer was waiting outside the door and informed me as I entered that my food was waiting for me inside. We ate dinner at the table in Keylan's kitchen, while I chattered happily about how excited I was to train with laserswords.

My trainer had never let me use any real laser or plasma weapons, since she was afraid I would hurt myself. She assured me that, if the need arose, I would be able to use the weapons thanks to my training. I personally had my doubts, which is why I was especially anxious to train with a real lasersword.

"Hey," I said as I finished my dinner, "what are we going to tell everyone if I end up getting hurt?"

"You're not going to get hurt." He assured me.

"I could." I shrugged.

"If you are with me," he said, "you are not going to get hurt." He stared intently into my eyes.

"You can't control it." I chuckled lightheartedly.

He grabbed my hands tightly, his eyes boring holes in my head. My eyes widened in surprise.

"I will do every single thing I can to keep you completely safe," he reassured me, "whatever I can control, I will."

"Keylan, if anything ever happens to me," I squeezed his hands, "please don't blame yourself."

He furrowed his brows and pursed his lips at my words.

"Please," I pleaded, "for me. I don't want you to have any more guilt or pain than you already have."

He released my hands and leaned back; his attention turned to his food.

"No promises." He sighed.

"Just try your best." I chuckled.

I watched Keylan closely as he finished his dinner. As soon as he took his last bite, I hopped up and grabbed his hands. He frowned as I yanked him to his feet before he could swallow his food.

"Let's go, let's go!" I shouted.

"Okay, okay." He laughed.

I nearly dragged him down the hall, not caring if anyone saw us. I was so excited to use laserswords I didn't even care if my parents caught me holding hands with the Commander and dragging him down the hall.

"Okay, where are they?" I bounced, looking around the training room.

Keylan stepped over to a safe by the wall which had been brought to Asphoamist by the Supreme Order; he unlocked it with a few biometric scans and a code. I watched with great interest as he pulled out two laserswords. One had a long silver and black hilt, with a knife-like glass blade and red plasma lining. The other had a medieval style grey hilt with a black polycarbonate fiber blade, which was also lined with red plasma.

My fingers buzzed with excitement as I reached for the first, with the knife-like blade. It looked just like the laserswords I had seen on holoprograms; the ones that slashed through diamonds as if they were nothing but paper.

"No." Keylan scolded, handing me the other.

"This is a kid's lasersword." I pouted, motioning to the custom blade guard that had been placed around the blade.

"It's a training lasersword," he corrected, "my first one, actually."

"You think I can't handle a proper lasersword?" I frowned.

"Not yet." He smiled.

I frowned and took the training lasersword from Keylan's hands. I twirled it a few times, getting a feel for the weapon. It was very heavy, which I did not expect from the way Keylan was carrying it. I looked back over at him and noticed that the black tank top and pants he was wearing perfectly explained why this had been; he was absolutely *ripped.*

"Are you ready to start?" he smirked.

I cleared my throat as I raised my gaze to meet his reluctantly.

"Yeah." I squeaked, suddenly nervous.

"Well, you obviously know the basic twirl," he commented, "what about the reverse twirl?"

He demonstrated it, his arm muscles contracting as he did so. I found myself gulping as I watched him show me the move. He motioned to me with his other hand, waiting for me to copy his movements.

I did know the reverse twirl, because it was the second thing I had ever learned. However, watching him do it made me feel nervous, and I clumsily copied his movements. He set his lasersword down and moved to help me; within seconds he had corrected me so that I was doing it better than I had ever been able to before.

"There, you got it!" he encouraged.

"Because you helped me." I chuckled.

"I had one of the best lasersword trainers in Soturna," he said, "and it took me at least a day to get it as perfect as you just did."

"Well, I've done it before," I shrugged, "I just... I've never been very good at it until you helped me."

He smiled and picked up his lasersword.

"Ready for the next one?" he offered.

"I guess." I sighed.

I suddenly felt really embarrassed; he was *amazing* at this, and I felt like a beginner, even though I'd done these moves with fencing swords a million times before.

"Infinity pattern twirls." He showed me.

It was another simple move, but I just knew it was going to be more difficult with the heavy lasersword. I tried to gracefully twist it as he had but failed.

"It's all right," he said, "it's a more advanced move with a more advanced weapon... it may take some time for your body to get used to it."

I groaned and turned off my lasersword. I collapsed to the ground, rubbing my eyes in frustration.

"I can do this with a fencing sword!" I groaned, "why am I failing so badly?"

"It's heavier and more awkward than a fencing sword," he returned, "but you'll learn to adjust.... here, watch how I move to account for the weight when I do it."

He demonstrated once more, this time going slowly. I studied his motions diligently, making mental notes of how he held the lasersword and twisted it so that it didn't burn him. I stood up and tried to copy his movements slowly. When I finally got it, I jumped up and down, almost dropping the singing blade on my toes.

"There you go!" he grinned.

"I got it!" I celebrated.

"You did." He nodded.

"Okay, let's do something else!" I suggested.

"No, no," he retorted, "we're going to practice real-life application of the moves now."

"Boring." I sighed.

He shook his head at me and ignited his lasersword. As if threatening me, he twirled the lightsaber and stepped towards me. I mimicked his movements, making a face at him as I did so. Taking advantage of my silliness, he did an infinity twirl towards me, forcing me to block him. A few little moves later, he had overpowered me and grabbed my waist to pull me close to him. As he leaned in to brush his nose to mine, I hooked my legs behind his knees and forced him to the ground.

I circled around him, the blade of the lasersword inches from his neck. I smiled deviously as he extinguished his lasersword and threw it to the side. I giggled happily as I faced him, holding the lasersword between us. Then, I turned it off and tackled him, knocking him on his back.

"Hey!" he protested.

"I got you." I said.

"Only because you cheated." he argued.

"I did not cheat," I disagreed, "I merely slipped out of your grasp."

He rolled his eyes at me and pushed up into a sitting position. I wrapped my legs around him, holding onto him like a koala bear.

"You know, we probably should have closed the privacy shields." I noted, turning my head towards the glass walls.

"It's more exciting this way." He returned.

"How so?" I questioned.

"The thrill of the possibility of getting caught." He smirked.

"Whatever." I scoffed, pushing off him.

He pushed me over onto the floor and pinned me down.

"Hey!" I whined.

"Don't let your guard down." He warned.

"But I beat you." I returned.

"If I'm not dead," he said, "I'm still a threat."

"So, you want me to kill you?" I mocked.

"Kill your enemies." He pushed off me.

"All of them?" I inquired.

"All of them." He nodded.

I bit my lip and furrowed my brows; I didn't want to even think about killing my enemies, or anyone for that matter. I wanted to stay in the protected bubble that I lived in now. I once thought I longed for adventure and excitement, but now that I thought of it, I realized I wanted to stay home and safe.

"Don't worry about it," Keylan smiled, noticing my anxiety, "I'll protect you."

I blushed as he brushed a strand of hair behind my ear. I wanted to reply that I would protect myself, as I always did, but I didn't know if I wanted to. Maybe it wasn't so bad, letting *him* protect me; I had never wanted a man to protect me as a matter of pride, but Keylan wasn't so bad. I was still perfectly capable of protecting myself, but it was nice to be able to rely on him.

"I know." I replied.

I yawned, only now noticing how tired I was. Keylan seemed to notice as well, since he stood to pick up both laserswords. As he put them away, I collapsed back on the floor.

"Keylan?" I called him.

"Yes?" he replied.

"Are you really the best lasersword fighter in the world?" I asked.

"I guess." He chuckled.

I wondered if there was truly any way to test such a thing.

"Do you think I could ever beat you?" I questioned, "when you're not going easy on me, I mean."

"You will be able to," he smiled, looming over me, "if you do exactly what I tell you."

I reached my arms up to him and allowed him to pull me up. He lifted me effortlessly and I stumbled back onto him.

"How did you get so good at this stuff?" I asked.

"Years of practice." He answered.

"So, it's going to take me years to get as good as you?" I frowned.

"I don't know," he said, "you've obviously done some stuff that will help you improve quickly... and you have a great teacher."

I nudged his torso with my elbow.

"Can we train again tomorrow?" I asked excitedly, turning to face him.

"Your parents are going to have private meetings with the Senator and Senatress all day tomorrow," Keylan told me, "So, we can train all day if you want to."

I hadn't heard about these private meetings, but I didn't care; I just cared about training with Keylan.

"I want to." I smiled.

"Well, we'd better to get to sleep then," he said, "because we're going to train our butts off tomorrow."

I giggled and nodded happily. Even though lasersword fighting with Keylan was exhausting, I found it exhilarating. Maybe if he trained me, I could become as good as him in half the time.

Keylan took my hand and lead me back to his rooms. Upon arriving, I sent my personal officer to get me a nightgown while Keylan went to shower and change. I was secretly envious of the fact that the guest rooms had showers. The royal bedrooms had the standard, traditional bathtubs since Leader Syphex was so obsessed with us taking our time with every aspect of our lives. The Supreme Order Dignitaries were allowed to rush through things, like the common folk were, so as not to waste any time.

My officer came back quickly, and I was able to change before Keylan came back out into the bedroom. I snuggled down into the soft sheets and awaited his strong arms to pull me close to him. I fell asleep with a huge smile on my face, dreaming only of lasersword training with Keylan.

I woke up before Keylan the next morning. I turned over and stared at his beautiful face, completely peaceful as he slept. I brushed his dark hair out of his eyes before turning to see what time it was. When I saw the time, my eyes widened in shock. It was 0800, which meant my halcyns, *not* my officers, would be guarding my rooms. Silently cursing my sleepiness, I got up and straightened my dress and hair. I decided not to wake Keylan, since he seemed so blissfully calm in his sleep. I gathered up my clothing from the day before and tiptoed quietly out of his rooms. My personal officer had done me a favor in not telling my personal halcyn that I was inside Keylan's rooms; the halcyn would be waiting for me back at my rooms.

"Azalyn?" The voice made me freeze in my steps.

After the shock had worn off, I turned slowly to see one of the last people I would have wanted to see me exiting Commander Keylan Rixar's rooms holding my clothes in my arms. I grimaced, trying to find a reasonable excuse.

"Joyriak, I..." I started.

"It...it's him...it's...it's the Commander." She stammered.

I hushed her, looking around to make sure no one else was around.

"What are you doing here?" I whispered.

"I could ask you the same thing!" She retorted.

"I'm sorry, I wanted to tell you," I apologized, "but I couldn't."

"I thought...I thought it was the General." She stuttered, her hand flying to her forehead.

"I know, but you were wrong," I said, "now can we please go before someone else catches me?"

Her hand stayed on her forehead as I dragged her back to my rooms. Seeing Joyriak by my side, my halcyns did not question where I had been the night before. Instead, they let us glide right into my rooms. I pushed Joyriak down onto the couch in my sitting room and went to fetch her a glass of water.

"Here." I handed her the water, sipping my own as I studied her.

"You were…you were carrying clothes." She stated, as if thinking through everything.

"I was." I nodded.

"Oh, God help me," she looked towards the sky, her hand flying to her heart.

"What?" I frowned.

"You didn't get the northern travel shots, did you?" she queried, tears filling her eyes, "you got something else and you... and he... and you!"

"What? No!" I laughed, "that's not why I was carrying clothes." I blushed.

"Then... then why?" she hyperventilated.

"He was training me last night," I explained, "with laserswords." She sighed in relief.

"So, you two are not romantically involved?" She smiled.

"Well, we are, but…" I stumbled, "we didn't…. this is so weird."

"You're dating the Commander of the Supreme Order?!" she screamed, rising from the couch.

"Shut up, would you?!" I hissed, pulling her back down on the couch, "do you want the whole castle to know?"

"I don't know, maybe!" She returned.

"Joyriak, you can't tell anyone," I said, "*we* can't tell anyone."

"And why not?" She scoffed.

"He'll get in trouble with Leader Syphex and the alliance will be ruined," I explained, "besides that, they'll separate us."

"I'm not sure that's a bad idea." She snorted.

I rolled my eyes at her and set my empty glass down on the coffee table.

"Can I not have a romantic relationship with someone?" I argued.

"Not with him." She replied.

"And why not?" I folded my arms over my chest.

"He's over 10 years older than you!" She said, "not to mention he's the Commander of the Supreme Order!"

"And I'm the Cerulea of the Asphoamist Kingdom, what's your point?" I returned.

"He's dangerous, Azalyn." She told me.

"How so?" I interrogated.

"You know the things he's done." She said.

"To people threatening Soturna." I argued.

"Aza, if he hurts you, I will not be able to restrain myself," she warned, "I will hurt him in whatever way I can and I will be executed for it."

"He's not going to hurt me." I assured her.

"He's never hurt you?" She stared into my eyes.

"Never." I said.

She continued to search my eyes, looking for any indication that Keylan had hurt me; I knew she wasn't going to find what she was looking for. Maybe he had gripped me too tight once or twice, but he had never intentionally hurt me either physically or emotionally. His main concern always seemed to be protecting me, so why would he ever hurt me?

"I want to speak with him." She announced finally.

"What about?" I questioned.

"You." She replied.

"Joyriak, he's the Commander of the Supreme Order." I whispered.

"And your boyfriend." She added.

"Fine," I relented, "but I'm staying with you."

"Now that that's out of the way," she sighed and lounged back into the couch, "tell me everything."

I relived the entire story of our relationship to her before my sphoas came to get me ready. We made plans to meet up directly after breakfast in my rooms so we could walk to Keylan's rooms together. I was dreading it, especially since this would reveal to Keylan that someone knew about us, but I knew she wasn't going to give up.

"Aza, are you okay?" Lorne queried at breakfast.

"Yeah, of course," I beamed, "why wouldn't I be?"

"You seem…on edge." He commented.

"Just tired, I guess." I shrugged.

I really was quite tired. Not only was I emotionally drained from talking to Joyriak about Keylan, but I was exhausted from last night's training; Keylan was certainly going to keep me on my toes. I hurried back to Joyriak after breakfast, making excuses to Lorne. I felt bad that he would be spending the day alone, but I knew Joyriak would go to Keylan's rooms without me if I wasn't there soon. She was waiting by my door when I arrived, ready to go. I made her wait for me to change into training clothes before we left, which she begrudgingly did. We linked arms as we nearly flew down the halls toward Keylan's rooms.

The officers, whom I assumed knew about this morning's incident, let us in immediately. Keylan emerged from his bedroom, wearing only a pair of black sweatpants. I could tell from his clothing, or lack thereof, and his expression that he had only expected me.

"Cerulea Azalyn." He greeted me formally, straightening up.

"Drop it," I sighed, "she knows."

"You told her?!" he snapped.

"She caught me." I shrugged.

Joyriak stared up at Keylan defiantly, her shaky hands the only thing betraying her emotions. She walked closer to him and squinted at him; she looked him up and down, then stepped back.

"As Azalyn's best friend, I feel I should warn you," she said, "if you ever hurt my Aza, in any way, shape, or form, I will personally murder you. Brutally."

"Okay, Joyriak." I pulled her arm.

"I expect nothing less." He smiled.

She nodded, obviously taken aback but impressed.

"Joyriak, can you go keep Lorne occupied?" I requested, "Keylan and I are going to have a lasersword training session in the gym and I don't want him catching us, too."

"I'll keep Lorne occupied forever." She blushed.

"Thanks." I smiled, embracing her quickly.

Joyriak scurried out of Keylan's rooms, glancing back at Keylan once more. She gestured to him that she'd be keeping an eye on him before the doors slid shut behind her. Keylan's deep chuckle echoed throughout the room, making me relax.

"She's a good friend, I like her." Keylan commented.

"She is." I beamed.

"At least I know if I can't protect you," he said, "she will."

He smiled, pulling a black tank top over his torso.

"All of my alysseas will." I returned.

We walked side-by-side to the gym, where we closed the privacy shields. It certainly was exhilarating to have the threat of someone catching us looming over our heads, but we realized we couldn't risk it. We were lucky enough that Joyriak didn't run to my parents.

As I predicted, Keylan kept me on my toes the entire training session. He showed me a few new moves, then made me practice them in a mock-fight. This time he did not let me win as easily, causing me to ache as I tried to hold my ground. When he finally had mercy on me and knocked me to the ground, I begged for a water break. He obliged, laughing as I crawled back to my gym bag.

"Shoot." I muttered as I checked my holophone.

"What's wrong?" Keylan plopped onto the ground next to me.

"My parents summoned me to their sitting room 15 minutes ago." I groaned.

I put my things back into my bag and fixed my hair quickly.

"I'll see you as soon as I can, okay?" I kissed Keylan quickly before standing and grabbing my bag.

I stumbled out of the gym, already sore from today's workout. I wondered if I would ever truly be able to keep up with Commander Keylan Rixar. After today, it did not seem like I would.

"Azalyn." My mother greeted me.

"Mother, father." I nodded, sitting on one of the couches.

"You were training?" My father queried.

"Yes," I responded, "that's why it took me so long to get your message."

"Well, no matter," my mother beamed, "we wanted to ask you a few questions."

The color drained from my face. Had Joyriak told them? Or given them hints? Had they figured it out their own? I tried to hide my anxiety as they stared at me. I nodded, unable to speak for the moment.

"Are you and Lorne still getting on well?" My father interrogated.

"I believe so." I answered.

"And do you like him?" My father continued.

"Yes, he's a very fun person to be around." I replied.

My parents shared a brief smile, confusing me further.

"Do you think, perhaps, you will keep speaking to him after he's left?" My mother asked.

"I suppose, if he wants to." I shrugged.

"I think you should spend some more time with him today…get to know him better." My mother added.

"Why?" I wrinkled my nose involuntarily.

"Because he is a member of the visiting Senatorial Family," my father said, "it is good for the alliance we hope to form with their kingdom."

"Of course," I nodded, "I'll be sure to spend time with him this afternoon."

My parents responded to this gladly before essentially kicking me out of their rooms. I noticed it was nearly time for lunch, so I went straight to Miransi's rooms. Our parents decided not to join us, so I told her all about how odd they were acting. She suggested that we might be close to making an alliance, and that a friendship with Lorne would solidify it. I doubted this but couldn't find another reasonable explanation, so I decided to accept this one.

After lunch I sent Joyriak, whom I could now trust to be a messenger for Keylan and me, to tell my boyfriend I would be unable to see him until dinner. I decided not to offer an explanation, thinking it would be better if he didn't know what I was doing. Joyriak offered to distract him, but I knew he would immediately know what she was up to and get suspicious. So, I simply went off to spend time with Lorne without taking any precautions.

I had to get dressed in a proper outfit, since I couldn't show up at Lorne's rooms in workout clothes. As soon as my dressing was finished, I trudged straight to his rooms. I knocked slowly on his doors, partially hoping he wouldn't answer so I could go train with Keylan. To my dismay, he answered almost immediately.

"Aza!" He grinned.

"Did you want to hang out for a while?" I offered.

"Sure!" He exclaimed, exiting his rooms.

"Is there anything you wanted to do?" I inquired.

I certainly hoped there was something he wanted to do, because I had absolutely nothing planned.

"Actually, there is," he admitted, "could we go dance in the dance studio?"

"You dance?" I asked in surprise.

"Yeah," he chuckled, "we use to dance together when we were little."

"Oh, I don't remember." I confessed.

"That's okay," he laughed, "I didn't expect you too."

I lead him to the dance studio, which was currently empty. I typed a quick message to Joyriak to subtly round up the alysseas and bring them here; I really didn't want to dance alone with Lorne.

"What do you like to dance to?" I asked, flipping through songs on the holospeaker.

"Can I?" He motioned to it.

I stepped back, allowing him to pick out the song. He stopped on a song and stepped to the side so I could see; it was an old Latin song that I'd danced to with my alysseas once or twice.

"We had a choreographed dance routine we used to do to it," he recalled, "I still remember it…I could teach it to you again. Although, we should probably update it now."

"My alysseas and I have choreography to it as well." I informed him.

"Huh," he smiled, "well, maybe we could have a competition later."

"Yeah," I shrugged, "they're actually scheduled to be here in an hour or so anyways."

"Well then, we'd better get to work." He said, pushing play.

It didn't take me long to learn the choreography he had apparently updated. It was fairly simple, but still showed off his dancing skills. I had to admit, I was thoroughly impressed. I hadn't expected him to be more than decent, but he was actually quite good. He was also more energetic than I had originally guessed.

"There!" He exclaimed after we finished a rehearsal of the dance, "see? We've got it!"

As if on cue, my alysseas shuffled into the dance studio. I greeted them kindly, sweating and panting from the exercise. They stretched and warmed up as Lorne took me through the choreography one last time.

"So, girls," I announced as they joined us on the dance floor, "today we're going to be having a competition."

They cheered excitedly.

"Lorne and I will be doing our choreography to one part of this song" I explained, starting the song so we could assign portions of it, "while we do our choreography for the rest of it."

"I'll be judge." Vyri offered.

I nodded, understanding that she was nervous to dance in front of a stranger. She took her place by the mirrored wall and once we had assigned our portions of the song, she restarted it with the remote. My alysseas and I started off the song, then they scurried off as Lorne approached for his part. They cheered us on good-naturedly, then joined me for the ending of the song.

"Wow!" Vyri exclaimed as we finished.

"So, who won?" I asked.

"They were both amazing, but…" she said, "Aza, you and Lorne DEFINITELY won today."

My other alysseas groaned in mock disappointment, then congratulated us.

"You up for another dance?" Lorne questioned.

"Do you mind splitting the floor?" I turned to my alysseas.

"Not at all!" Daska replied cheerfully, sharing a glance with Vyri and Saalia.

Vyri hit the button on the remote to bring the divider in. I jokingly waved goodbye as the divider slid between us. Once it was closed, Lorne suggested another old Latin song.

"Te gustan las canciones en Español?" I joked.

"Si, bonita." He replied with a wink.

"You speak Spanish?" I laughed.

"I *am* Hispanic." He smirked.

"Oh, I didn't know." I giggled awkwardly.

He chuckled at me and went off to play the music.

"Sing with me?" He requested.

"No." I replied shortly.

"Canta conmigo." He pleaded.

"No!" I retorted.

"Por favor, princesa?" He pouted.

"Ugh, fine." I relented.

We sang the song together as he guided me through choreography he seemed to be improvising. He tried to get me to continue conversing in Spanish despite my constant protests.

"Shut up and dance." I finally commanded, rolling my eyes.

He laughed and obeyed my command. After the song was over, he walked me through the choreography, which seemed as if it had been planned before this moment. I considered asking him how long he'd been creating this choreography but thought better of it.

"Sing while we dance." He ordered.

"No!" I protested.

"Come on, you have a great voice." He pleaded.

"I'm seriously going to kill you." I warned before I began singing.

I hated how weak my voice sounded as I tried to keep up with the choreography. Even though I wouldn't admit it to anyone, I was thoroughly exhausted. I'd been training with Keylan for most of the morning and now I'd spent my entire afternoon dancing. The announcement for dinner was a welcome one.

"I have to get ready for dinner." I told him.

"Hasta luego." He pressed a gentle kiss to my hand, not breaking eye contact.

"Hasta luego." I chuckled, hurrying off.

I wore yet another one of the revealing dresses gifted to me by some visiting dignitary, wanting to impress Keylan.

"Cerulea Azalyn, do you want me to order you some new dresses?" Xamie asked.

"No, why do you ask?" I frowned.

"I'm sorry, Cerulea, it just seems as though your style has changed." He apologized.

"How so?" I inquired, checking my reflection in the mirror.

"You seem to prefer dresses with less...coverage now." He answered.

"It is getting quite hot here." I noted.

"Yes, Cerulea," he replied, "do you want me to order you a summer wardrobe with less coverage so you will not be too warm?"

I bit my lip, thinking for a bit. Would I really need more revealing clothes? Keylan seemed to be impressed with me regardless of what I wore.

"Not right now," I finally answered, "I'll let you know if I think I need more."

"Yes, Cerulea." He bowed out, leaving me to look myself over in the mirror.

Once I was happy with my appearance, I strutted out of my rooms. I felt confident and elated as I walked into the dining hall. Again, all eyes were on me as I entered. Lorne pulled my chair out for me, pushing it in gently as I sat down.

"So, Azalyn," my mother began, "what did you and Lorne do today?"

"We went to the dance studio and danced for a few hours." I smiled.

"Did you have fun?" Senatress Varros questioned.

"Yes." I smiled.

"I always have fun with Azalyn." Lorne added.

"I'm afraid you have had a poor sampling of fun in your life." I joked.

"That's exactly what I thought when I met you." He returned.

Our heads turned towards the sound of Keylan's helmet hissing as he pressed the release buttons. He slid it off his head, revealing his raven-black locks. His dark eyes avoided me, and his lips stayed pressed firmly together.

"I hope you all enjoyed your day off." My father addressed the Supreme Order Dignitaries.

"Yes, Lumin." Captain Plutan answered on their behalf.

We began eating the first course, an awkward silence permeating the room. I looked over at Lorne, who had to hold in a laugh as we shared a look. I cleared my throat in an attempt to hide my own laugh.

"Azalyn." My mother addressed me.

I looked up, thinking I was about to me scolded for my badly hidden emotions.

"I think perhaps you and Lorne should continue practicing your dancing." She suggested.

Senator and Senatress shared a look at this statement. I saw Lorne frown at them out of the corner of my eye.

"Um...why?" I stuttered.

"No reason." My mother smiled, looking at my father with a knowing look.

I furrowed my brows and glanced over at Lorne, who mirrored my expression. I shook it off as the chalis set the next course in front of us. Polite conversation was made as usual, and dinner was finished without any more awkwardness.

After dinner, Lorne grabbed my attention and began talking about some new dances he wanted to do. Meanwhile, Keylan threw on his helmet and stomped out of the dining hall. I seemed to be the only one who noticed, as everyone continued to chatter cheerfully around me.

"Maybe we could talk it over in your rooms?" Lorne asked.

"Sure." I replied, not really paying attention to the conversation.

"All right, let's go!" He exclaimed, grabbing my hand.

I reluctantly followed him back to my rooms, noticing the expressions of our respective parents. They seemed a little bit too excited about us going to talk in my rooms. Perhaps they wanted us to become good friends for the sake of the alliance. Or perhaps they were preparing us to take over and form an alliance ourselves.

"So, what did you want to talk about?" I plopped onto my couch.

He sat beside me, making himself rather comfortable.

"Some more songs we could dance to." He said.

He gave me an odd look and I remembered he had talked about this earlier, I just hadn't been paying close attention.

"Okay...which ones do you want to do?" I queried.

I tuned him out as he began listing a plethora of songs.

"And I thought maybe we could do some more floor work?" He finished.

"Huh?" I responded.

"More floor work...for the duets?" He repeated.

"Oh...uh, sure, if you want," I shrugged, "you're the one doing the choreography."

"You can do some too, if you want." He said.

"No, it's okay," I chuckled, "I'm not very good at choreography anyways."

"Well, I'll go get started on it, okay?" He beamed.

"Yeah, I'll see you tomorrow." I smiled.

"Awesome, see you tomorrow!" He waved as he exited my rooms. I sighed in relief; glad I didn't have to find out an excuse to get him to leave. I glanced at my watch and saw that he had, somehow, been in here for nearly two hours. My eyes widened in shock. I hadn't realized he'd ranted about dancing for nearly two hours.

"I'm going to Keylan's." I informed the officers quietly as I left my rooms.

They nodded in acknowledgement as I hurried to his rooms. He was obviously bothered about something, probably the fact that I'd had to cut our training session short. I hoped he wasn't too offended that I'd spent the afternoon with Lorne.

Keylan's officers moved aside as I approached the door. The door slid open immediately and I stepped into the well-lit room. I looked around, searching for Keylan.

"Keylan?" I called out.

I heard his heavy footsteps approaching from the bedroom. Keylan emerged, wearing only black sweatpants. His dark hair was soaked, and he was drying it with a small towel. I gulped as I took in the sight of him. A smirk flashed across his face before he resumed his stern look.

"Huh…how…how are you doing?" I awkwardly placed my hands on my hips.

"I was great until I saw you dancing with *that boy*." He sneered.

"You saw me dancing with Lorne?" I questioned.

"Yes." He replied, turning his back to me.

I studied his muscular back as I tried to form words.

"How?" I coughed, trying to regain my composure.

"General Armande, Captain Plutan, and I walked around the castle," he informed me, "we stopped by the viewing room."

"How did we do?" I beamed, averting my eyes as he pulled a shirt on.

He turned back around and glared down at me. I shifted my eyes away, wondering what was wrong with him now.

"Fine…you dance much better with him than you do with me." He spat.

"Uh…okay?" I stuttered.

"Do you like him better than me?" He rambled, "do you like the young boy with the pretty face?"

"Are you seriously jealous of him…again?" I raised an eyebrow.

"Of course not." He retorted.

"You so are!" I argued, "how many times do I have to tell you that I love you and only you?"

He didn't respond.

"Why are you so jealous of him?" I questioned.

"Because he's young and talented and handsome!" He yelled.

I was taken aback by his response. He noticed this and turned back around, hiding his flushed face.

"You're much better than he is, in a lot of ways," I returned, "which is why I love you and not him."

He didn't turn around or respond.

"You saw how my parents are pushing us together," I continued, "I need to stay close to him so we can form this alliance."

"But you don't need to flirt with him." He turned, his face red.

"I'm not flirting with him," I said, "I'm being friendly."

He frowned, considering my words.

"He doesn't see it that way." He told me.

"How would you know?" I folded my arms over my chest.

"It's painfully obvious," he crossed the room, "he's falling for you."

I frowned, considering his words now.

"I'm sorry." I apologized.

"It's not your fault…it's his." He sighed.

"When can we tell people about us?" I questioned.

"Probably not until after we're married." He chuckled, wrapping his arms around me.

"Well, can we get married now?" I groaned, burying my face in his chest.

"I told you, you're not ready yet." He whispered, stroking my hair.

I growled in frustration, knowing he was right. As much as I wanted to be, I wasn't ready for marriage. Even though I didn't want to wait a second longer, I would have to.

"I'm tired," I manned, "can we go lay down?"

"Sure." He pressed a kiss to the top of my head before leading me to bed.

I snuggled into his warm chest and drifted off into a deep sleep within seconds.

Chapter Eighteen: The Enigma

At breakfast the next morning, my parents shifted nervously in their seats. I studied them diligently, wondering what they were up to. I also noticed that the Senator and Senatress seemed to be quite anxious about something.

"Now that breakfast is finished," my father stood, "we have an announcement to make."

"Will you please join us on the main balcony?" My mother smiled. Everyone filed out of the dining hall and onto the main balcony, where Miransi was awaiting us. Her expression told me she didn't know what this was about, either.

"Good people of Asphoamist," My mother spoke to the crowd gathered below us, "we will be throwing a ball tomorrow night to celebrate the Senatorial Family."

Everyone clapped politely and I saw Lorne smile at me out of the corner of my eye. I kept my eyes focused on my parents' backs, not wanting my expression to betray my emotions. I was confused as to why they were throwing a ball now and why my parents seemed to be pushing Lorne and I to practice our dancing. Did they really expect us to dance that much at the ball? Was I expected to dance with him a lot because it was technically in his honor?

"We should get working on our dances!" Lorne exclaimed, linking arms with me as we filed off the balcony.

"I have to go meet with my alysseas first, to make sure I don't have to do anything to prepare for the ball today." I returned.

"Of course…do you want to meet up for lunch?" He suggested.

"Uh, sure…just come to my rooms and you can eat with me and my alysseas." I answered.

"Okay, I'll see you then!" He waved as he jogged off towards his rooms.

Once everyone else had cleared out of the hall, I turned to Vor'en.

"Go to my rooms and tell Shula and Kaxdan to call Joyriak," I commanded him, "she needs to begin my preparations for the ball tomorrow. I have an errand to run."

"You don't want me to accompany you, Cerulea?" He inquired.

"There are halcyns, officers, and alysseas everywhere," I smiled, "I'll be perfectly safe."

He bowed and hurried off towards my rooms. Once he was out of sight, I scurried off to Keylan's rooms.

"You know I'm going to have to spend a lot of time with Lorne tomorrow." I said, not even greeting Keylan as I entered his rooms.

"I know." He growled.

"Why are they throwing a ball for the Senatorial Family now?" I folded my arms over my chest.

"I don't know." He groaned, rubbing his face with his hands.

I frowned at his obvious frustration and annoyance.

"Am I annoying you?" I asked, feeling a bit irritated myself.

"No…this….ugh!" He exclaimed, knocking something off the kitchen table.

"Hey, what's wrong?" I approached him slowly.

"Something's going on, but I have no idea what," he admitted, "your parents aren't telling us anything…you know the Senator and Senatress are too scared to talk to us."

"So, they're not letting you in on whatever they're doing?" I questioned.

"No." He growled.

"Well, me neither." I chuckled.

"Yeah, but it's different." He argued.

"Because I'm younger than you?" I scoffed.

"Because you're their child...I'm their superior," he returned, "we're forming an alliance with them, and we were here first. We deserve to know what's going on between your two families."

"I'm sure they'll tell you when the time's right," I assured him, "why are you getting so upset?"

I saw his jaw clenching and unclenching.

"Hey." I reached up and turned his head towards me.

"I just want to know what's going on," he sighed, "if they're...if they're doing something I want to know."

"Everything's going to be okay." I reassured him.

"I know." He kissed my hands gently.

My watch buzzed and I looked down at it. Joyriak had messaged me, summoning me back to my rooms.

"I gotta go…Joyriak needs me." I told him.

He nodded.

"I'll see you at dinner." I called back to him.

I rushed through the halls back to my rooms. Inside were all my alysseas and sphoas, flitting around as they tried to quickly get everything ready for tomorrow's ball. Joyriak hurried to my side, wrapping her arm tightly around mine. She leaned in close to me, obviously wishing not to be heard by anyone else.

"You were with him, weren't you?" She hissed.

I glanced over at her but didn't say anything. I knew that after all our years of friendship, she knew my answer from just one glance. She sighed and nodded, obviously displeased with me.

"I need you to dance with Lorne a lot tomorrow," I told her, "Keep him distracted."

"Is your *boyfriend* getting jealous?" She spat.

"He thinks something's going on between our two families," I informed her, "until we figure out what's going on I need to keep my distance from him."

"Do you think it's something bad?" She frowned.

"No…not necessarily." I responded.

"Do you need me to find anything?" She whispered.

In the past, Joyriak had been a very good spy for me. She and Shri-Lan were especially talented at finding out political information and secrets for me. Meanwhile, Vyri, Daska, and Saalia could always get the best social information and secrets for me. Padalynn was more straightforward in her approach, mostly because she was so shy and quiet that she often went unnoticed. This made each of my alysseas valuable in bringing me important information.

"No," I shook my head, "we'll all know eventually."

"Maybe they're close to forming an alliance." Joyriak suggested.

"Would my parents make an alliance with them before the Supreme Order?" I asked, "they were here first...wouldn't it be considered rude? Especially since the Supreme Order is higher up than Waskaura?"

"I don't know," she shrugged, "the Supreme Order was just on a mission...maybe the threat of Canada is worse than we think. Maybe your parents will make alliances with whoever they can, whenever they can, no matter the consequences."

"I doubt they'd be that foolish." I frowned.

"Desperate times call for desperate measures." She replied.

"Do you think…do you think I could form an alliance between our kingdom and the Supreme Order?" I inquired, "by…through other means?"

Her eyes widened and she pulled me inside the bathroom. No one paid us any mind, too involved in getting my things ready for tomorrow. She locked the door behind us and moved towards the farthest wall so we wouldn't be heard outside.

"Is that why you got the shots?" She hissed, "so you could marry him?"

I simply gulped and nodded, unable to say anything.

"Has he…has he proposed already?" She gasped.

"No…I….I proposed the *idea* to him," I explained, "he says I'm not ready yet."

"You're not," she agreed, "wait…repeat what you just said."

"What? He says I'm not ready yet?" I frowned.

"He...*he* said exactly that? That *you're* not ready?" She interrogated slowly.

"Yeah…why?" I raised an eyebrow.

"Has he ever said that he's not ready?" She pressed.

I furrowed my brows, trying to think about every time we'd talked about marriage.

"Not that I remember." I shook my head.

"Well, he's either a better guy than I've heard," she said, "or he's making excuses and he's an absolute player… which is doubtful… you know, considering."

"What do you mean?" I inquired.

"He said you're not ready," she said, "which implies not only that he is, but that he cares enough about you and your wellbeing to suppress his desires… or like I said, he's a huge jerk trying to avoid commitment. But you claim you haven't broken your vows, so I do doubt he would play that game at this moment in time."

I chuckled nervously, processing the information. I racked my brain for all our conversations about marriage. Remembering how melancholy he seemed when speaking about marriage, I realized she could be correct with her first guess.

"Wow." I breathed, trying to process the information

"Okay…we can talk about this later," she said, "we need to get back out there."

She dragged me back out to my bedroom, where everything was starting to wind down. Vyri and Saalia had picked out my dress for tomorrow and were waiting impatiently for me to try it on. The dress they had chosen for me was my absolute favorite. It was a beautiful blue color and had a huge skirt that accented the small, corseted bodice. The sleeves were ruffled and off-the-shoulder while the bodice boasted a golden design on the front.

They all gasped as I emerged from my dressing room in the dress. I twirled happily, feeling like a proper princess. I absolutely could not wait to wear this to the ball.

"You look gorgeous, Aza." Joyriak complimented me.

"You'll have the whole kingdom in love with you!" Daska exclaimed.

"So, this is the one?" I beamed.

They all nodded enthusiastically.

"Okay, let me go change so we can get it ready for tomorrow." I smiled.

I really did not want to take off the dress. It was truly the most beautiful thing I had ever worn, which was saying something considering I was a princess. I felt ethereal when wearing it and I hoped I looked just as good. My alysseas hungrily took it from me as I emerged from the dressing room and began making slight alterations.

"We're going to add a shorter skirt underneath," Ginovae told me, "And make the big skirt detachable."

"That will make it much easier for you to do more complex dances." Erri added.

"Perfect!" I grinned.

A knock sounded from the door, and we all turned towards it.

"Uh, come in." I stammered, wondering who was here.

Lorne stepped into the room. I sighed, trying to hide my disappointment. I then looked down at my watch to confirm that it was, in fact, lunchtime.

"You're all excused for lunch." I informed them.

Everyone bowed out except for Joyriak, who was being tightly held

to my side. Not only did I not want to be left alone with Lorne, but I

also wanted her to have some time with him. I felt guilty enough

spending a lot of time with him.

"Your other alysseas aren't staying?" He asked nervously.

"I wanted to discuss some matters which are not appropriate for

everyone else's ears." I answered.

He glanced over at Joyriak.

"Joyriak is my most trusted friend and alyssea," I explained, "she

knows every single thing about me, my family, and the current

situation."

He nodded and I motioned to the coffee table. Lorne sat in an

armchair across from the couch I chose to sit at with Joyriak.

"Joyriak, would you mind ordering our lunch?" I turned to her.

"Of course." She smiled, nervously folding her hands in front of her.

"What is it that you wanted to discuss, Azalyn?" He inquired,

fidgeting anxiously.

"I want to know if you know why the ball is being thrown." I told

him.

"I thought it was to honor my family." He frowned.

"Yes, but you've all been here for several days," I continued, "besides, our parents have been in a lot of private meetings lately."

His gaze shifted to Joyriak, who had returned to my side.

"Do you know if there is something going on that I don't know about?" I pressed him.

"You know as much as I do, Aza." He shrugged.

"Have your parents mentioned anything to you? Or acted different?" Joyriak joined.

"Not that I recall." He shook his head.

"Lorne, we're becoming good friends," I said, "will you promise to tell me or Joyriak if you notice or hear anything?"

"Of course." He assured me.

"I'm trusting you, Lorne," I informed him, "not many people get that privilege."

"And those who lose the privilege often regret doing so." Joyriak added.

I was surprised by her sudden confidence around Lorne but attempted to hide it. Usually, she would get flushed and nervous around him, but she seemed to be her usual self around him now. I wondered if it was just because I was with her.

"I promise to tell you everything I find out." He reassured us.

I smiled at him as chalis served our lunch. We made polite conversation over lunch, trying to avoid the previous topic as much as possible. I could tell he felt uncomfortable talking about political topics, so I didn't want to push him too far.

"Azalyn, I was wondering if we could practice some of our dances for tomorrow?" Lorne questioned as we finished lunch.

"Do I have time?" I asked Joyriak.

"Yeah…we'll get everything taken care of." She smiled.

"All right…come get me if you need to." I squeezed her hand.

I exited my rooms with Lorne, slightly excited about getting a break from ball preparations. I would have liked to dance with my alysseas or do lasersword training with Keylan better, but dancing with Lorne would suffice.

"We're not plotting against you." He blurted out as we walked.

"I know that." I furrowed my brows.

"I just…you seemed like you thought maybe we were going to betray your family." He stumbled.

"I don't think that at all," I assured him, "I just want to know what's going on between our two families."

"I do too." He nodded.

"And I really want to make sure our families do not insult the Supreme Order." I continued.

"Are they insulted?" His face drained of all color.

"I'm sure they're not." I reassured him.

He nodded nervously, remaining silent for the remainder of the walk. I wondered if I had offended him or scared him. I hoped not, as I much preferred him when he was comfortable and talkative than when he nervously sputtered out a rant now and then.

"Did you come up with some new choreography?" I smiled as we entered the studio.

"Yeah! I think it's going to be great!" He exclaimed, seeming to melt back into his comfortable state.

"Great." I beamed.

Lorne slowly walked me through the new choreography, seeming to be especially excited about the floorwork in one of our dances. I knew it would probably make Keylan angry, but Lorne was incredibly proud of his work, and I didn't want to hurt his feelings. We worked on the new dances as well as the old dances until I was stolen away by Joyriak for dinner.

"How was it?" she asked cheerfully.

"It was okay." I shrugged.

She smiled and nodded.

"Hey…you're not mad at me for spending time with Lorne, right?" I clarified.

"Not at all," she frowned, "why would I be?"

"You're the one with the crush on him." I nudged her gently.

"You two are just friends…just like we are," she assured, me "I don't mind you two spending time together at all."

"You tell me if you ever do mind." I ordered her.

"I trust you, Aza." She smiled.

A great weight was lifted off my shoulders. I had feared I was spending too much time with Lorne and that I was becoming too friendly with him. Keylan certainly seemed uncomfortable with our closeness, which is exactly why I wanted to clear things up with Joyriak.

"Are you excited for the ball tomorrow?" she inquired cheerfully as she helped me dress for dinner.

"I'm excited to wear that pretty dress and to dance." I shrugged.

"And what are you not excited for?" she pressed.

"I'm not excited for all the unnecessary socialization and political conversation." I chuckled.

"As usual," she laughed, "but I'll be with you as usual, too."

"I know," I beamed, "hey…did you want to sleep over tonight?"

"Are you planning on sleeping in your rooms tonight?" She raised an eyebrow.

"Yeah…there's too many chalis around for me to sneak out." I shrugged.

"Sure!" she smiled, "I'm going out to eat with Padalynn but I'll come back as soon as we're done."

"Awesome, I'll see you later." I waved as I hurried to the dining hall. After dinner, I hurried back to my rooms and called for my sphoas to ready me for bed. Joyriak came in soon after I was done, and we began our sleepover by watching some of our favorite holoprograms. The night with her was relaxing, free from political worries or drama. It was just as it had been before the Supreme Order Dignitaries and Senatorial Family arrived. Only us two, holoprograms, and snacks, snuggled on the couch in my sitting room.

Chapter Nineteen: The Senatorial Ball

"Cerulea Azalyn, Cerulea Azalyn!" Erri shook me awake.

"You shouldn't have slept on the couch, Cerulea," Xamie scolded, "it's bad for your skin."

"I know…I'm sorry." I apologized, "I must have fallen asleep watching *Blue Sea and Sky* last night."

I went through my normal morning routine, then had my breakfast brought to me by my alysseas, who had come to share the day's first meal with me. We chattered happily about the upcoming ball as we ate. Immediately after we were finished, I was grabbed my sphoas and forced to sit for various treatments. Beside me, my alysseas copied the treatments on themselves while talking to me about all the latest news.

"Oona Quo told me she heard the Canadians sent soldiers to attend the ball tonight." Vyri whispered to us.

"Vyri!" Joyriak scolded.

"What?" Vyri furrowed her brows.

"You're going to scare Aza half to death." Joyriak continued.

"Oh…sorry Aza." Vyri blushed.

"It's okay…do you think Oona was telling the truth?" I inquired.

"You know Oona…she's probably making it up or misheard it."

Joyriak reassured me.

"She thought it was true." Vyri shrugged.

"Should we make preparations for Azalyn's protection?" Shri-Lan

asked the rest of the girls.

"I don't think it would be a bad idea." Padalynn looked over at me.

"Don't worry too much about it, let's just have fun tonight." I

smiled.

"Aza, why don't you let Shri-Lan, Padalynn, and I make

preparations?" Joyriak placed her hand atop mine.

"I don't want you all to miss out on the ball." I replied.

"We'll be too worried about you the whole time." Shri-Lan

interjected.

"Are you sure?" I looked over their faces.

"Daska, Vyri, and Saalia are the party girls," Padalynn laughed, "you

know we don't mind missing a ball every now and then."

"If you're sure." I nodded.

They smiled and nodded in response, before hurrying out the door. Vyri, Saalia, and Daska tried to keep me distracted with other news, but the anxiety was gnawing at me. The last ball we'd had was followed by the assassination and injury of our Senatorial Family. If Vyri's friend was right, this ball could be followed by a similar situation.

"If Oona was right," I blurted out during an awkward silence, "who do you think the Canadians are going to go after next?"

"She probably wasn't right." Saalia responded with a comforting smile.

"But if she was, who do you think they'd try to assassinate next?" I pressed.

The three of them shared a nervous look.

"Me? My family?" I tried to swallow the lump in my throat.

"It's possible," Daska answered, "but there's no way we can know. They could go after the Senatorial Family of Waskaura or even the Supreme Order Dignitaries."

"Are you sure you don't want us three to plan for your protection too?" Vyri asked.

"No…it will be okay, I'm sure." I forced a smile.

"We're not going to let anything happen to you or your family." Daska assured me.

"I don't want anything to happen to you girls either." I returned.

"That's our job." Saalia shrugged.

"I don't care about your job…you girls may have started out as just my alysseas," I said, "but you all became my closest friends and I love you all."

"We love you too," Daska smiled, "which is why we're going to protect you if anything happens."

I smiled back at her before I was whisked away by a sphoa to begin getting dressed for the ball. After my dressing, hair, makeup, and finishing touches were completed, I stepped back into my sitting room. Joyriak, Padalynn, and Shri-Lan were back, looking less anxious and melancholy than I had expected. They all fawned over me, and I returned their praises as I looked over their completed looks.

"Aza, we retrieved some of your halcyns," Shri-Lan told me, "they're going to be accompanying you tonight."

"I'll stay by your side as much as I am able to," Joyriak continued, "Shri-Lan will be walking behind you outside of the ballroom and will follow you during the ball."

"And I'll stay in front of you. I've got a dress similar to the shorter version of yours underneath my dress," Padalynn added, "I'll act as your decoy if anything goes wrong."

"Please try to enjoy the ball as well," I urged them, "I really don't want you worrying too much about me."

"We will." They answered in unison.

We assumed the formation and walked out of my rooms, buzzing with excitement and nervousness for the ball. I entered with my family as usual and greeted the Supreme Order Dignitaries. The Senatorial Family entered after us and I greeted them as well.

"Lorne, why don't you ask the Cerulea to join you for the first dance of the evening?" Senatress Varros suggested.

"What do you say, Azalyn?" He offered me his hand.

"I'd be honored, Lorne." I replied, taking his hand.

We walked to the middle of the dance floor, and I realized we were one of few couples there. There would be no risk of us being overheard.

"I heard something." I whispered as we began the dance.

"What?" He frowned.

"Oona heard that Canada has sent some soldiers to be here tonight," I informed him, "presumably in disguise."

"Sorry, who's Oona?" He queried.

"Oh, right, sorry," I laughed, "I guess I got carried away with my news."

I looked over to see Shri-Lan watching us from the crowd that surrounded the dance floor. Joyriak stood a few feet away from her, surveying the room carefully.

"Oona is friends with Daska, Vyri, and Saalia." I explained.

"Your alysseas?" He clarified.

"Yes." I replied.

"Is she a reliable source of information?" His eyes flitted about the room.

"I don't know, I've never met her." I admitted.

"So, she could be lying." He said.

"I guess, but we can never be too careful." I returned.

"That's certainly true." He chortled.

I smiled at him as the song ended. He offered me his hand as the next song began. I took it, not thinking about how I should probably dance with one of the Supreme Order Dignitaries to seem respectful.

"I'll protect you if something happens." He winked.

"I don't need you to protect me." I snapped.

"Oh, I'm sorry…I know…I know that." He stammered.

"I'll protect you." I raised an eyebrow.

"I'm sure you will." He laughed.

I laughed as he spun me around the dance floor. As we danced, I caught a glimpse of Keylan and the rest of the Supreme Order Dignitaries. Both he and Captain Plutan had foregone their helmets, which comforted me a bit. If they felt safe enough to come to the ball without helmets, then we were probably relatively safe. Although Keylan had an indifferent facial expression, his body language revealed his true feelings. I realized I really should have made my way over to them after dancing with Lorne. In fact, I should not have danced with Lorne first; the Supreme Order Dignitaries outranked him by far.

"I should go ask the Commander to dance," I said as the song ended, "I don't want to offend the Supreme Order."

"Of course." Lorne bowed.

I curtsied before hurrying off to the Supreme Order Dignitaries. I greeted them politely before asking Keylan to dance. He begrudgingly accepted and we waltzed out onto the dance floor. I noticed a few of the couples move away from us as we took to the floor.

"What were you two talking about?" Keylan asked coolly, his jaw clenched.

"A rumor I heard." I responded.

"About?" His gaze shifted from Lorne to me.

"My alysseas' friend mentioned something about Canadian soldiers being here tonight." I told him.

He frowned down at me.

"I think it's just a rumor, but after what happened last time..." I drifted off.

"Your alysseas have a plan?" He inquired, looking around for them.

"Joyriak, Padalynn, and Shri-Lan formulated a plan earlier today." I responded.

"Did you bring weapons?" He interrogated.

"No." I frowned.

"After the ball go straight to your rooms and have your alysseas stay

with you," he demanded, "have Joyriak and an officer walk you to

the gym tomorrow after dinner."

"Why?" I queried as the song ended.

"Cerulea, may I have the next dance?" Hanew interjected.

"Of course, General." I smiled cordially.

I shot Keylan a glance as he stormed off the dance floor.

"Is everything okay, Azalyn?" Hanew questioned, "you seem very

troubled."

"I suppose I'm just worried about the looming threat of Canada," I

forced a laugh, "I'm very happy to have the ball as a distraction."

"You look beautiful tonight." He complimented.

"Thank you, sir." I beamed.

"As I said at the previous ball," he smiled, "you *can* call me Hanew

if you'd like."

"Okay…Hanew." I grinned.

He chuckled, sending a rush of glee through me. Although he was a

very strict and professional man, he had a fun side. He somehow

made me feel at ease in social situations like this. I definitely felt

closer to Lorne and Keylan, but I still considered him a friend.

"I want you to come directly to me if you have any problems with Lorne or the Commander." He said.

"I will." I nodded.

"Might I have the next dance?" Captain Plutan interjected as the song ended.

"Of course." I answered.

I curtsied to the General, who bowed to me before leaving. Out of the corner of my eye, I saw Daska grab him. He soon escorted her onto the dance floor, and I nearly rolled my eyes at her blushing face.

"Are you enjoying the ball so far, Cerulea?" Plutan inquired.

"Yes, are you?" I returned.

"Yes." She smiled.

I knew she was only dancing with me to be polite and because Shri-Lan was otherwise occupied. I could tell from her glances that she would much rather be dancing with Shri-Lan right now.

"I'm afraid there have been rumors of a threat from Canada tonight," I explained, "so some of my alysseas have taken protective measures."

"Oh?" She turned back to me.

"Yes…I'm sure they'd much rather be dancing," I chuckled, "but they insisted on focusing on my protection tonight."

"I do hope nothing happens that would require action from them." Plutan replied.

"I hope so, too." I agreed.

After the song ended, I was whisked away by Keylan once more. He remained silent as we danced, seeming rather distracted. His grip on me was tight, almost bruising my skin.

"Are you going to tell me why you want to meet at the gym tomorrow night?" I finally asked.

"You'll see when you get there." He responded shortly, his eyes flitting about the room.

"What's wrong?" I frowned.

"I want you by me or one of your alysseas all night." He said.

"You know I can't do that." I returned.

"Try your best." He demanded, turning his gaze to me.

"You don't really think there's going to be an attack tonight?" I questioned.

"We can't be too careful." He shrugged.

"I shouldn't have told you anything." I sighed.

"You should always tell me if you think you're in danger." He retorted.

"I don't think I'm in danger! It's probably just a rumor!" I exclaimed, a bit too loudly.

He stared deep into my eyes, seeming to be silently scolding me. I rolled my eyes and focused on the rest of the dance. I was tired of everyone being worried about me. Every single person that I'd told about the threat tonight, except Captain Plutan of course, had expressed their unnecessary concern for my safety.

"Cerulea, can I have this dance?" Lieutenant Chasta interjected immediately after the song ended.

Keylan glared down at him, but Chasta paid him no mind. Chasta simply beamed down at me and offered me his hand. I nodded and took his hand, glancing back up at Keylan quickly. Keylan stormed off the dance floor, pulling Hanew aside.

"You look very beautiful tonight, Cerulea." Chasta complimented.

"Thank you." I answered cordially.

Lieutenant Chasta awkwardly made polite conversation as we danced. He was quite a clumsy dancer, but I was able to handle his mistakes well. When the dance was finally over, Keylan approached us rapidly.

"Lieutenant, I need to speak with you outside." Keylan growled through his teeth.

He shot a look at me, silently reminding me of his earlier order. I gave him a small nod before hurrying over to Joyriak. Lieutenant Chasta followed Commander Rixar out of the ballroom, looking exceptionally pale.

"Is something wrong?" Shri-Lan questioned, glancing over at the pair.

"Don't know." I shrugged.

"Did you need a break from dancing?" Joyriak offered with a smile.

"Yeah." I laughed.

I spent the 7th and 8th songs with my alysseas, turning down any offers I received with grace. I wanted to wait until Keylan was back safely before I began dancing again. Joyriak realized this and kept an eye on the door for me. When he returned with a sheepish Chasta, she nudged me in the ribs. I turned my attention to Keylan, who stalked over to me and simply offered his hand. I took it immediately and followed him onto the dance floor.

"What happened?" I queried.

"I had to put the Lieutenant in his place." He replied.

"Why?" I questioned.

"He should not have asked you to dance when you were dancing with me." He told me.

"So, when is he supposed to ask me?" I furrowed my brows.

"When you are dancing with someone of the Captain's rank or lower," he explained, "or when you are not dancing with anyone."

"Since when is that one of the Supreme Order's rules?" I scoffed.

"It's not an official rule…more of an unspoken rule." He retorted.

I rolled my eyes at him. I loved him, but sometimes he could be a bit full of himself.

"But nothing's wrong? That's all you talked to him about?" I clarified.

He nodded, his eyes beginning to scan the ballroom again.

"You need to relax." I said.

He frowned down at me, obviously not planning on obeying my command. The song ended and he kept his grip on me.

"You go get a drink, I'm dancing with the General." I brushed him off of me.

"You are not dancing with *him*." He spat.

"What is he going to do in public?" I questioned, "go get a drink and relax."

He growled before stomping off towards the refreshments table. Meanwhile, I approached the General and asked him for another dance. He again made polite conversation, keeping me engaged the entire time. He nearly distracted me from Keylan's intense gaze, which hovered on me from the refreshments table.

"General, may I steal the princess from you?" Lorne approached us as the song ended.

"Certainly." Hanew replied amicably.

Lorne stole me from everyone for the next two songs. He chattered happily about our upcoming opportunity to show off the dances we had performed. I indulged him in cheerful conversation, forgetting momentarily about the rumored threat.

"Do you remember the song I taught you when we were little?" He inquired.

"What's it called?" I frowned.

"*La Llorona*...it's a Mexican folk song." He replied.

"Oh, I remember that!" I exclaimed, "by the way, I forgot to ask you. How did your family become the Senatorial Family of Waskaura if you're from Raeganar?"

"My parents moved to what used to be California before I was born." He shrugged.

"Huh." I nodded.

"Anyways, I was going to ask if you'd sing it for everyone?" He queried.

"Sing?" I furrowed my brows.

"I want you to sing *La Llorona* with me on stage," he beamed, "please say yes, because I already asked your parents if you could and they think you're singing."

I groaned and rolled my eyes at him.

"When?" I moaned.

"Uh…right now." He chuckled nervously.

The last song of the formal hour ended with me staring wide-eyed at my friend.

"Really?!" I whispered.

"I'll be with you the entire time." He squeezed my hand reassuringly.

Ithan announced the end of the formal hour as well as my upcoming performances to the crowd. Everyone gasped excitedly and clapped. Lorne dragged me to the stage, constantly assuring me that everything would be fine. He led me to the microphone placed at the center of the stage, then stepped off to the side. Finally, he motioned for me to begin and gave me a reassuring nod.

I began the song, my voice sounding odd without backing music. After the first two lines of the song, I heard the strumming of a guitar. I looked over to Lorne, who was playing the accompaniment for me. I furrowed my brows at him, wondering why he'd never told me that he played guitar.

As I continued to sing, looking over at Lorne every so often for encouragement, I began to feel the music. I gained confidence as I looked over the crowd, all politely paying attention to me. The orchestra behind me began to play along with Lorne and I, giving me a surge of boldness.

A music break occurred, and I motioned for Lorne to come closer. He obeyed, bringing his guitar with him. We swayed to the music, laughing brightly, and I began to sing once more. As I began to sing the chorus, Lorne put his guitar aside. When I repeated the first line of the chorus, he began to sing with me. I stared at him in shock, barely able to keep singing. He had sung softly with me during dance practice, but he never sounded very good. Now, he sounded like an angel from Heaven.

He smirked at me as I let him take the last portion of the song. The mischievous twinkle in his eyes told me that this was his plan the entire time. He wanted me to be shocked onstage in front of everyone like this. As soon as he finished the song, I playfully swatted his arm. He feigned hurt before motioning for me to curtsy to the audience. I curtsied, then motioned for him to bow. He gave the crowd a half-bow before turning back to me.

"Lorne!" I scolded him as we descended the stage stairs.

He laughed as he avoided another playful hit from me.

"I never said I was going all out in the dance studio." He smirked.

"You are a jerk and you are only allowed to talk to me tonight if you go get me some water." I folded my arms over my chest.

"Yes, my princess." He responded with a playful tone, bowing mockingly before fulfilling my request.

"Azalyn! You were great!" Vyri ran towards me with Daska and Saalia in tow.

Out of the corner of my eye, I saw Joyriak, Shri-Lan, and Padalynn move cautiously towards me. Their eyes scanned the room, as if making sure there was no threat before approaching me.

"And, Lorne was too!" Daska fanned herself.

"Hey, I called dibs." Joyriak smiled.

"Well, you better hurry if you want him." Saalia smirked.

Lorne approached me with two cups in hand. He handed one to me before greeting my alysseas. They all responded with a polite smile before sharing a knowing look.

"Do y'all want to go dance?" I asked after finishing my water.

They all answered in the affirmative and we hurried out onto the dance floor. We danced to the music cheerfully until the next song began.

"Our song!" Vyri squealed.

"We should do what we did for the competition!" Saalia exclaimed.

I looked over at Lorne, who shrugged and grinned.

"Let's do it!" I agreed.

The dance floor cleared a bit as we all performed the dance. Lorne, to my surprise, danced along to our part as well. Then, when it came to our part, he stole me from everyone. My alysseas cheered us from the sidelines, then stole me from him once more.

As the song finished, the crowd surrounding us began to applaud. We bowed to them, trying to suppress our giggles. By some miracle, the next song was one that Lorne and I had choreography to. In fact, the next two were songs we had choreography to. I wanted to ask him if he had arranged this as he had arranged us singing but didn't have time to do so between the dances.

When there was finally a song we didn't have choreography to, I made a breathless excuse to him and hurried off to my alysseas. They complimented me warmly and I thanked them as I grabbed water from a passing chali; I was thoroughly tired from keeping up with Lorne's fast-paced choreography.

The next song began, and I could have sworn that Lorne had bribed the chalis in charge of music. He motioned for me to join him for the song, which we of course had choreography for. I tried to plaster a smile on my face as I performed the dance with him, but I felt exhausted. I couldn't wait until social hour when he wouldn't be able to drag me out on the dance floor anymore.

"The last one!" Lorne shouted breathlessly.

I nodded as the last song we had choreography to played. I danced along with him, a surge of energy coming from the thought that this was the last song I'd have to dance with him to. Unfortunately for me, this song had the most floor work involved, and Keylan just happened to be watching. I knew he wasn't going to like what he saw.

The last dance Lorne and I performed left the crowd in astonished awe. My parents and Lorne's, to my surprise, looked pleased instead of cross. The choreography was a bit risqué, especially for a political ball, but everyone seemed impressed. Except for Keylan, of course. Joyriak, who was diligently watching me and looking slightly hurt, followed my gaze. She looked at Keylan, whose face was red and whose fists were clenching and unclenching rapidly. She looked back at me, nodded, and hurried towards him.

"I'm going to go see Joyriak." I excused myself quickly.

We met each other right by Keylan.

"Commander, will you escort us? I'm afraid we forgot something in my rooms." I looked up at him.

He hesitated for a moment, his jaw clenching and unclenching in unison with his fists. I feared that he would either say no or would lose his temper in the middle of the ballroom. A sigh of relief came from both Joyriak and I when he finally nodded. I took Joyriak's arm and we scurried out of the ballroom, closely followed by Keylan.

I lead them down a secluded hallway away from the ballroom before stopping and turning back to Keylan. Even in the darkness, I could tell how furious he was. The little light that illuminated our faces showed me that his was still burning with anger.

"Would you like to explain why you just made a fool of yourself in front of everyone?" He growled.

"I thought we danced well." I shifted uncomfortably.

"Yes, you danced very well," he scoffed, "and very sensually…with a man you are not in a relationship with."

"You're seriously jealous that I danced with my friend at a ball?" I rolled my eyes.

Keylan's eyes shifted to Joyriak. I turned, following his gaze. She looked extremely uncomfortable.

"Joyriak, do you think that the dance performed by Lorne and I implied anything more than friendship?" I crossed my arms over my chest.

I knew she wouldn't lie to me. At least, not directly. We were the best of friends, and we would never lie to each other.

"Joyriak?" I repeated when she did not answer immediately.

"Um….it was…" she stammered, "it was quite…intimate."

"So, you both think there's something going on between Lorne and I?" I inquired, looking between the both of them.

I knew the answer even though they did not respond to my question.

"All right, listen," I took a deep breath, "Lorne choreographed it and I don't know why he chose to do it the way he did, but I liked it and I thought we did well. I have zero interest in being anything but friends with him and he seems to feel the same well. Keylan, I am in love with you and only you. Joyriak, I know your feelings towards Lorne, and I would never go after him because of that."

"If you…if you do like him, it's okay with me." Joyriak smiled sadly.

"I don't, I promise," I reassured her, "I do like him very much as a friend, but nothing more."

I looked towards Keylan, who seemed to be tearing up.

"Speaking of which," I chuckled, "why don't you go distract him, Joyriak?"

"I'm not sure he wants to be distracted by me, but I'll try." She laughed nervously.

"Where is my confident Joyriak?" I teased, "you know that you are beautiful, and charming, and intelligent. Go show him how amazing you are."

She smiled and giggled, hugging me quickly. I then shooed her away and she ran off towards the ballroom. As soon as she was out of sight, I turned back to Keylan. A couple of tears had escaped his eyes and were rolling down his cheeks. I stepped closer to wipe them away.

"You know, every time you got jealous, I got kind of pissed at you." I chortled, "I thought you were being all angry and controlling."

He shifted his gaze away from me, focusing on the stone walls surrounding us.

"I'm sorry if I made you think I'm not in love with you," I apologized, "and I'm sorry if I hurt you."

"I'm sorry that I'm so jealous," he chuckled, "it's just…he's so much younger and probably better for you. You would be able to have a healthy relationship with him that you wouldn't have to hide."

"As soon as the alliance is formed, we won't have to hide anymore." I assured him.

Keylan smiled down at me and pressed a quick kiss to my forehead.

He held me close for a few moments and I melted into his embrace.

"You go back first." He finally said.

"Okay." I nodded.

He kissed my knuckles before releasing me to hurry back to the

ballroom. I smiled when I saw that Joyriak and Lorne were deep in

conversation, grinning at each other as they talked. This smile faded

when Lorne noticed me and rushed towards me, away from Joyriak.

My heart dropped as I saw Joyriak's face drop. I motioned with my

head for her to come over and she obeyed.

"Aza!" Lorne exclaimed.

"Hey, Lorne." I responded.

Joyriak floated to my side, linking arms with me gently.

"I was thinking maybe we could perform one more duet tonight?"

He queried, "the last song of the transitional hour?"

"What song would we do?" I returned.

"The one we did during dance practice." He replied.

"It already played." I said.

"It'll be different when we sing it." He chuckled.

I turned to Joyriak.

"What do you think?" I asked her.

"You both have lovely voices," she beamed, "I'm sure everyone here would be glad to hear you two sing again."

"I guess it won't hurt to sing one more song." I shrugged.

"It's settled then!" He exclaimed happily.

He grinned at both of us before hurrying off to make the arrangements. Joyriak sighed mournfully and took a sip of her drink once he was out of earshot.

"What is it?" I interrogated her.

"He likes you, Azalyn." She told me.

"No, he doesn't," I scoffed, "he likes you. You two were getting on so well."

"Before you came in." She laughed sadly.

"We just spend more time together so he's more comfortable with me," I assured her, "besides, who would want me when they could have the wonderful Joyriak?"

She rolled her eyes playfully at me.

"Cerulea, I was wondering if you'd join me for a dance?" The General's voice sounded behind me.

I turned to face him with a courteous smile.

"I'd be delighted, Hanew." I responded.

I took his arm and he led me to the dance floor. I was almost glad that he'd asked me to dance again. At the last ball we had spent so much time together, but at this one I had been floating between Lorne, Keylan, and my alysseas.

"Are you tired of me already?" He joked.

"No," I chuckled, "why do you say that?"

"You seem quite troubled." He observed.

"I suppose I'm just worried about political things." I sighed.

"Don't worry too much for tonight." He smiled.

"I'll try not to." I replied.

"I forgot to congratulate you on a splendid performance," he continued, "you have such a beautiful singing voice, I didn't know."

"Thank you." I blushed.

"Do you sing often?" He questioned.

"When I'm alone." I giggled.

"Well, you are a very talented singer," he complimented me, "in fact, you sound as if you are a professional singer…perhaps you should consider a career in music rather than in politics?"

"General, are you implying I am not capable of being a decent Lumina?" I raised an eyebrow.

"On the contrary, I think you are more than capable," he retorted, "I simply think you have one of the loveliest voices I have ever heard." I blushed and looked at our feet, moving together perfectly to the music. The way we synced and got along so well sometimes made me wonder if I should be with Hanew rather than Keylan. I did love Keylan, of course, but it seemed almost as if Hanew and I were better suited. He did not seem as passionate or jealous as Keylan, though I couldn't judge his character well just yet.

"One more dance, my Cerulea?" He offered.

I nodded happily, accepting his offer. I wanted a bit of time alone with the General.

"Hanew, I've been meaning to ask you about something." I stated nervously.

"Yes?" He responded.

"Do you think there's any possibility I'll be able to intern at the Supreme Order Base?" I asked, "That perhaps I'll be able to leave with you and the other Supreme Order Dignitaries?"

"Do you want to leave with us?" He breathed.

I nodded, lost in his intense gaze.

"Are you anxious to stay with me, Azalyn?" He smirked.

"I'm anxious to see the Supreme Order base." I retorted with a playful grin.

"I'm doing my best to get you an internship this fall." He answered.

"Will I work closely with the Supreme Order Dignitaries?" I inquired.

"I'll see to it that you will be with us as often as possible." He smiled.

"Why are you so kind to me, Hanew?" I questioned.

"I like you, Azalyn," he replied, "you are strong and intelligent…exactly what the Asphoamist Kingdom and Soturna need."

Out of the corner of my eye, I saw Joyriak motioning for me to come to her. The music ended and I saw a chance to take my leave.

"Hanew, will you excuse me?" I smiled, "I'm afraid I have to go speak with my alysseas."

"Until the next time." He bowed his head.

I gave him a slight curtsy before hurrying towards Joyriak. She clutched my arms tightly, pulling me close. Padalynn and Shri-Lan moved in around me, effectively blocking me from everyone else.

"What's wrong?" I whispered.

"Commander Rixar ordered us to retrieve you." Joyriak responded.

"Is something wrong? Is there a threat?" I pressed.

"He says." Shri-Lan scanned the crowd.

"Shri-Lan, Padalynn, why don't you two go scout the area?" I suggested, "Joyriak will stay with me as my guard."

The pair shared a look before nodding and hurrying off. I pulled Joyriak closer to me so we could talk without being heard.

"Is there really a threat or did the big baby just get jealous?" I hissed.

"I don't know," she shrugged, "he seemed very…alert."

"He is when he's jealous," I rolled my eyes, "do you think it's bad that he's this jealous? Do you think he trusts me?"

"We both trust you," she returned, "but you have three other guys flirting with you, so I understand why he's jealous."

"Three other…who is flirting with me?" I scoffed.

"Do you really not know?" She raised an eyebrow at me.

"No, I really don't know." I replied.

"Lorne, the General, and the Lieutenant." She answered.

"I've told you both before…Lorne and the General are just close friends," I breathed, "and I barely speak with the Lieutenant…how could he flirt with me?"

"Just be careful around them…both for yourself and for Keylan." She urged me.

Shri-Lan and Padalynn returned as we finished our conversation.

"Is all well?" I asked them.

"As far as we can see." Shri-Lan shrugged.

"Shall we go dance, then?" I continued, "I'm sure I'll be just as safe on the dance floor as I am in this corner."

"Perhaps one of us should stay behind, just in case?' Shri-Lan offered.

"You'll be able to protect me much better if you're with me." I returned.

She nodded, still seeming unsure, before scanning the ballroom once more.

"Go invite Captain Plutan to dance with us," I took her hands and squeezed them gently, "she seems very bored and lonely."

Shri-Lan looked towards Captain Plutan longingly.

"Go!' I urged her.

She smiled brightly before hurrying off towards Captain Plutan. Joyriak, Padalynn, and I giggled as we watched her nervously invite the captain to dance. We then stepped onto the dance floor to meet them as the next song began. After only two songs spent dancing with my alysseas, I was grabbed by Lorne.

"We should prepare to go onstage." He told me.

"Very well." I sighed, waving goodbye to my friends.

He dragged me towards the stage, where two microphones were being set up. I tried to hide my reluctance to be up onstage with him again as he squeezed my hand. When everything was ready for us, we took to the stage in preparation for the next song.

After a successful performance, we took our bows. I hurried off the stage, Lorne close behind me. Despite my attempt to escape him, he grabbed my wrist and pulled me back.

"We make a good team…we should do more duets." He smiled.

"Yeah…maybe." I laughed.

I wanted to get away from him as soon as possible. Although I enjoyed his company as well as singing with him, I didn't want to send the wrong message. Originally, I thought Keylan was just being overdramatic and jealous, but if Joyriak thought he was interested in being more than friends, I needed to be careful.

"Are you in a hurry?" He joked as he followed me through the crowd.

"I just want to get back to my alysseas." I excused myself.

"Is something wrong?" He inquired.

"Not that I know of." I answered.

I finally came to my alysseas, all huddled in a group. Lorne grabbed my hand again, holding me just inches from my friends.

"I was hoping I'd stay close to you during social hour." He grinned.

"Usually, one branches out during social hour," I informed him, "that is the point of the hour."

"Oh... I...I know that," he stammered, "but I don't really know anyone here and I was hoping you might introduce me."

"The Cerulea needs to stay close to those protecting her tonight," Joyriak came to my rescue, "but I'd be happy to escort you around for the hour."

"What a lovely idea, thank you Joyriak." I cut in before Lorne could respond.

He smiled politely and offered his arm to her. I silently thanked God that I had such an amazing friend before turning to my other alysseas.

"Any threats?" I questioned.

"Nothing." Shri-Lan told me.

"Why do you suppose the Commander told you all to retrieve Aza?" Vyri spoke up.

"Hush, Vyri!" Shri-Lan scolded her.

"I'm just asking a question." Vyri returned.

"Well, ask it more quietly." Shri-Lan demanded.

"Do you think there's a threat?" Saalia whispered.

"We didn't find anything suspicious." Padalynn informed us.

"He's probably just nervous." I shrugged.

"If he knows about the threat, what Oona said must be true!" Daska exclaimed.

"Not necessarily." Shri-Lan shook her head.

"I told him while we were dancing." I interjected.

They all looked at me with wide eyes.

"You told the Commander what Oona said?" Vyri queried.

"Yes…he is the second most powerful man in the nation," I said, "he should know what's going on."

"What else do you tell him about our conversations?" Saalia frowned.

"Nothing, really," I chuckled, "just things I think he should know about…like political things."

It was surprisingly true that I never revealed more than needed to Keylan. I tried to keep the conversations between my friends and I relatively private; him being my boyfriend did not change my loyalty to them.

"You didn't tell him that we thought he and the General are cute, did you?" Daska hissed.

"Of course not!" I giggled, "although I should."

"No!" Daska swatted my arm playfully.

I laughed at her slight panic and shook my head at her.

"Shri-Lan, do you think it's safe to mill about the room?" I interrogated.

"I believe so." She shrugged.

"But you should take us with you, just in case." Padalynn added.

"Very well…shall we go girls?" I beamed.

Padalynn and Shri-Lan linked arms with me while Daska, Saalia, and Vyri followed behind. They talked in hushed voices, mostly about their favorite ensembles of the night and the most attractive people in the room. Although I was glad they were enjoying themselves, I couldn't help but roll my eyes at them. All three of them were incredibly smart and talented, very capable of doing great things, yet they decided to occupy themselves with things like fashion and romance. I didn't look down upon them for it at all, but it certainly annoyed me at times.

"Your mother wants you to greet the Royal Family of Waskaura first." Padalynn told me.

"Are they here?" I whispered, "I thought after the assassination they decided not to visit."

"They're just stopping here for the night, then they'll continue on their tour." She continued.

"Well then, let's go." I sighed.

I had surprisingly never met the Royal Family of Waskauara. It was important that we meet them soon, though, since our alliance was in the final stages. I noticed that my family, as well as Lorne's, was already gathered around them.

"Ah, here she is." My father beamed as I arrived.

"Your highnesses." I curtsied.

"Cerulea Azalyn." The king greeted me.

"It's an honor to meet all of you." I smiled.

"Azalyn, this is King Brarton and his wife, Queen Jade." My mother told me.

I bowed my head and smiled at each of them in acknowledgement. King Brarton sat upon a beautifully decorated wheelchair and had a golden band around his head. He wore a long, dark orange skirt and a black top adorned with red and white designs. White marks adorned his cheeks, standing out against his tan skin. A tiny black ponytail rested atop his head, making him look almost like a pineapple.

Queen Jade seemed to be the opposite of her husband. Her dark hair and skin nearly matched her long, dark dress; the only thing that adorned her plain dress was a patterned belt tied around her waist. Also, she wore no face paint or crown like King Brarton. While the king seemed jovial and friendly, she seemed melancholy and serious.

"These are their children, the princes Preytan and Jorrar," my mother continued, "and the princesses Summer and Janta."

I smiled amicably at them, taking each of them in. I wished as I stared at the handsome princes and beautiful older princess that they were not already engaged. The oldest prince, Preytan, was set to marry Princess Raven of Raeganar. Meanwhile, Prince Jorrar was set to marry the Senatorial Daughter of Raeganar. They had met their future brides two years ago when they were working out an alliance with Raeganar; these marriages would solidify their alliance.

Princess Summer, the second eldest child and the eldest daughter, was going to marry a commoner girl from Waskaura. The girl she was to marry was said to be incredibly beautiful and intelligent; I wondered if she was even prettier than Summer was. Princess Janta was still too young to be engaged, but she seemed so bubbly that I wouldn't be surprised if she became engaged as soon as she hit adulthood.

"I'm so sorry I didn't greet you all earlier," I apologized, "I was under the impression that you wouldn't be coming tonight because of recent events."

"Don't worry about it, Cerulea," Jorrar chuckled, "we're just passing through."

"Perhaps I could make it up to you with a dance?" I offered.

"Unfortunately, we're leaving after the hour is over." Jorrar informed me.

"How unfortunate," I replied, "but hopefully we will be seeing you more in the future."

"Yes, Cerulea." King Brarton smiled.

My parents turned the conversation back to boring subjects such as the weather and recent political happenings. My alysseas shifted awkwardly behind me, shuffling away from our group to talk amongst themselves. At the soonest chance, I excused myself and rejoined my friends.

"Anyone else I need to see?" I turned to Padalynn.

"The Senatorial Family of Raeganar is visiting as well." She told me.

"Yes, I should greet them. Just the Senatress and James, right?" I clarified.

"That's right." She nodded.

After a lengthy conversation with Senatress Oata and her son James, I trudged back towards the Supreme Order Dignitaries. They had not branched out much during the hour and I knew it was my duty to engage with them if they were not otherwise occupied.

"Azalyn!" My mother walked quickly towards me.

I motioned for my alysseas to leave so that we could have a private conversation.

"Maima." I responded.

"I think you should go ask Lorne to dance." She smiled.

"Why?" I furrowed my brows.

"You two have been apart for nearly an entire hour." She returned.

"Is that a problem?" I asked.

"He is the visiting Senatorial Son of a kingdom we are trying to make an alliance with," she scolded, "who is about your age, no less! Talk with him, Aza."

"Yes, maima." I relented.

She beamed at me as I turned to retrieve Lorne from Joyriak. As if I didn't feel horrible enough about stealing him from her, I saw as I approached that they seemed to be getting along very well.

"I'm so sorry to intrude," I said, "Lorne, I was wondering if you'd like to dance the first song of the Companion Hour with me."

"I'd be happy to, Cerulea." He grinned.

I shot Joyriak an apologetic look as Lorne offered his arm to me. She gave me a reassuring nod before I took his arm. We stepped onto the dance floor, the first of a few couples to start dancing once more.

"Did you enjoy social hour?" I queried politely.

"I found myself in a few awkward situations, but Joyriak helped me immensely." He answered.

"She is very good with people." I commented.

"She is." He agreed.

"She is very beautiful and smart as well, don't you think?" I questioned, looking over at her.

"Yes." He smiled.

We danced in awkward silence for a few moments.

"You should ask her for the next dance." I urged as the song ended.

"Are you sure?" He frowned.

"Yes, she'd love to dance with you." I assured him.

"Cerulea, may I have this dance?" Lieutenant Chasta saved me just in time.

"Yes, Lieutenant." I grinned.

Lorne bowed before walking off towards Lorne.

"Lieutenant, I forgot to ask you if you've danced with Daska tonight." I stated.

"Unfortunately, I have not," he admitted, "we did not see much of each other after the last ball."

"I'm sure she'd love to spend some time with you tonight." I returned.

"Are you really sure?" He blushed.

"I am." I smiled.

As soon as the song was over, Keylan swooped in to save me. Lieutenant Chasta scurried away from us towards Daska.

"Why was the Royal Family of Waskaura here?" Keylan interrogated.

"He was just stopping by to see us on his tour." I responded.

"We were not made aware of their visit." He told me.

"Really?" I furrowed my brows.

He shook his head in response, his eyes wandering around the room.

"We'll have to talk to Leader Syphex about this tomorrow." He informed me.

"What for?" I snapped.

He locked eyes with me, his expression serious with a hint of worry.

"It is the duty of the Royal and Senatorial Families to inform the Supreme Order when they will be making visits like this," he said, "by not telling us, they have gone behind our backs."

"It's not that big of a deal," I laughed, "they just stopped by for an hour to see us."

"But why?" He questioned.

"I have no idea." I replied.

"If they have nothing to hide, why didn't they inform us of their decision to come here tonight?" He pressed.

I furrowed my brows in concentration as the song stopped. Hanew asked to cut in, to which Keylan replied with a formal nod. The General was not as preoccupied with political matters as his superior was. It was refreshing to talk about how good the food was or how pretty the stars were tonight.

"By the way, I'm not supposed to tell you this," he whispered, "but since we were just speaking out it earlier, I figured I should tell you."

"What is it?" I chuckled.

"Leader Syphex has approved your test to test out of levels 19 and 20 for September 1st," he grinned, "and he has also approved your spot as an intern on the Supreme Order base."

"Really?" I squealed, trying to contain my excitement.

"Yes, but you can't tell anyone I told you," he warned, "we've just been informed, and we aren't supposed to tell you until later on."

"I won't." I promised.

I chattered happily about how excited I was while Hanew nodded along, making comments here and there.

"May I steal the Cerulea back, General?" Keylan's voice sounded behind me.

"Commander, Cerulea." The General bowed quickly before turning on his heel to leave.

"A bit selfish of him to steal you for two songs." Keylan snarled

"It's my fault, I was talking too much." I confessed.

"About what?" He furrowed his brows.

"He gave me some good news." I smiled mischievously.

Keylan rolled his eyes and squeezed my hand tightly.

"He told you about the testing and the internship?" He growled.

"I didn't say that." I averted my gaze.

"But he did." He countered.

"Well…" I started.

"He's not supposed to tell you yet." He groaned.

"But he did. And you didn't." I raised an eyebrow.

"Because I know how to follow orders." He argued.

"And how to hide secrets from your girlfriend?" I returned.

"I wasn't hiding anything from you," he disagreed, "I was just waiting to tell you. I wanted it to be a big, special surprise. Not an afterthought at a ball."

"I appreciate the thought but I'd rather you just tell me immediately." I smiled.

"Next time." He nodded.

"I'm getting a bit tired," I said as the song ended, "I think I'll go sit with my alysseas for a bit."

"Do you need anything?" He inquired.

"No, I just need to sit for a song." I chuckled.

"I'll walk you to them." He offered.

I smiled and accepted his offer. I stumbled over to the bench where my alysseas were sitting, feeling quite sore from all the time spent on my feet. Keylan bowed and left once I was seated safely between Vyri and Saalia.

"These shoes are killing me." I whined.

"But they're so pretty!" Daska countered.

"That doesn't help the pain." I retorted.

After only one song, I was whisked away by Lorne for two more songs. He seemed to have gotten another burst of energy, as he talked the entire time. Keylan had either gotten jealous or saw me suffering and stepped in for the next song. Hanew stole me for one more song before I had to excuse myself to sit again. I kicked my shoes off, relishing the feeling of freedom from the tiny heels.

I was only given one song to recuperate. As soon as the Romance Hour was announced, Lorne was back. He seemed much too eager, making me want to throw one of my shoes at his feet. Not only was he proving Keylan and Joyriak right, but he was also hurting Joyriak and making me hurt my feet even more.

"This hour is so fun, no?" Lorne said.

I nodded in response, afraid I would cry if I opened my mouth. My feet felt as if they were bleeding right into my pretty new shoes. Lorne did not give me a chance to excuse myself, pulling me right into the next song. Keylan saved me from him, again seeming to seem my discomfort.

"My feet are dying." I confessed as soon as Lorne was out of earshot.

"Shoes?" He asked.

I nodded and bit my lip in pain.

"Well, Lorne's not going to let you sit a single song out, apparently."
He growled.

I chuckled, feeling a shot of pain go through my foot as I did so.

"Follow my lead." He whispered.

Keylan looked behind me at Joyriak and motioned subtly for her to
follow us. As he turned me across the floor, I saw her hurrying in our
direction. He swung me towards an empty bench and stopped,
swaying with me to the music.

"Kick your shoes under the bench." He commanded.

I obeyed his command, slipping the shoes off and under the bench.
Joyriak came right behind us, and Keylan nodded his head towards
the shoes. She nodded and picked them up, hiding them in her skirt
as she sat down on the bench.

"Okay, let's go back out there before Lorne steals you again." He
smirked.

I laughed as he spun me back out onto the dance floor.

"Here, step on my feet," he said, "it'll give you a bit of a break."

"Thank you." I beamed, stepping onto his leather boots.

"The good thing about this huge dress is that no one will be able to tell." He chortled.

"Right?" I giggled.

As the second song ended, Keylan noticed Hanew coming towards us.

"Just keep your shoes off…no one can tell." He whispered.

The dance with Hanew went remarkably well considering I was hurting and exhausted. He did make a remark about how I seemed a bit shorter but didn't seem to realize what had happened. As soon as the song was over, I was stolen by an overeager Lorne. Hanew did not seem pleased by his actions but walked away without saying a word.

After two songs dancing with a very chatty Lorne, I was asked to dance by Lieutenant Chasta. He nervously stammered about how he had talked to Daska and asked her to dance. I urged him to ask her for another dance, which he gleefully obeyed. I was again rescued by my boyfriend, who only kept me for two more songs before Lorne stole me once again.

I was a bit upset that I had danced with Lorne for the last two songs of the Romance Hour and the ball, but I knew he was probably being pushed by his parents as I was. As soon as Ithan announced the end of the ball, I said my goodbyes quickly and ran over to Joyriak. She helped me sneakily slip my shoes on before escorting me out of the ballroom with my other alysseas.

"Did you have fun tonight, girls?" Joyriak asked the group.

They all nodded happily before sounding out their favorite parts of the night. As we reached my rooms, they bid me farewell and split for their homes. After I was readied for bed, I peeked at the time. There was no way I was getting to Keylan's rooms tonight without getting caught.

I sighed and sunk down onto my couch. A gentle breeze blew the curtains against my window, seeming to call me outside. I answered by rising and opening the glass doors. The warm summer breeze blew my curls about my face, giving me a sense of peace. I closed the doors behind me and leaned against them, enjoying the warm air as I let my eyes close.

"Aza?" A deep voice drifted across the air.

I opened my eyes wide in shock to see Keylan gripping the balcony's stone railing. I rushed over to him, looking beneath and behind him anxiously.

"How did you get up here?" I asked.

"It was much too easy...you definitely need more guards." He frowned.

"What are you doing here?" I hissed, "someone could see you."

"I wanted to see you." He returned.

"We'll see each other tomorrow," I said, taking his face in my hands, "now you have to go before you fall and get hurt."

"Kiss me and I will." He smirked.

I rolled my eyes at him before kissing him quickly.

"Now go." I urged him.

"Fine." He groaned.

I watched as he climbed down the side of the building, much too quickly for my taste. When he was safely on the ground, he mock-saluted me and hurried off into the darkness. I watched him leave, my heart beating rapidly.

Chapter Twenty: The Rift

The next day brought a return to our usual schedule. Unfortunately, my body was not on the same page as everyone else's. I rudely fell asleep every few minutes, only to be awoken by Lorne seconds later. I tried to hide the fact that I was drifting off from everyone else, but I could tell by their looks that they all knew what I was doing.

Thanks to Lorne's assistance, I made it through the day. I didn't bother calling my sphoas to ready me for bed, deciding I would be better off sleeping in my underdress for the day. I also decided that it would be worthless for me to return to my own rooms, since I knew I would be with Keylan all night anyways. If anyone got suspicious, I now had Joyriak to help cover for me.

"You're early." Keylan noted as I stepped into his rooms.

"Nap first. Then talking." I responded as I collapsed onto his bed.

"Someone didn't get enough sleep last night, huh?" He chuckled.

"I hate going to balls." My complaint was muffled by the pillows.

"I don't," he sat on the bed next to me, "because it means I get to see you in pretty dresses."

"I always wear pretty dresses." I argued.

"But you wear *especially* pretty dresses at balls." He smiled.

I groaned and snuggled deeper into his bed. Understanding my lack of interest in continuing the conversation, Keylan helped me underneath the covers. As I drifted to sleep, I felt his warmth next to me and his hands stroking my hair gently. I sighed happily as I floated off into a deep sleep.

"What time is it?" I moaned as I blinked awake.

"2300." He answered, seeming distracted by his holopad.

"Oops." I giggled, pushing up into a sitting position.

"We should talk about the ball last night." He said, setting his holopad down to wrap his arm around my shoulders.

"What about it?" I inquired.

"We should figure out where your friend got her information from." Keylan answered.

"I told you, Vyri heard it from Oona." I shrugged.

"And where did Oona get her information from?" He pressed.

"I have no idea…they always say she's a bit of a gossip," I rambled, "she makes up things all the time…she was probably just trying to get people's attention."

"By scaring everyone?" He growled.

"She didn't mean it like that." I argued.

"Are you sure that your alysseas are loyal to you?" He turned to me.

"Of course I am!" I exclaimed, "they're my best friends…they would never do anything to me. I trust them completely."

"Maybe you should tell them to avoid Oona." He replied.

"Why?" I frowned.

"She may be working with the Canadians or involved with someone working with them." He told me.

"Just because you were betrayed by someone in your past doesn't mean that everyone's traitorous scum." I blurted.

I realized how awful my words were as soon as I said them.

"Oh, I'm sorry Keylan," I apologized, "I didn't mean…I didn't mean it like that at all."

"I know." He responded somberly.

I could tell by the way he tensed and drained his face of emotion that he was hurt. I furrowed my brows as I tried to think of a way to make up for what I'd said. I cleared my throat awkwardly before moving so that I could look straight into his eyes. I took his face in my hands gingerly, feeling like any rough movements could rip his heart.

"I promise I didn't mean anything by that," I continued, "you know I'd never say anything like that on purpose."

"It's okay." He feigned a laugh.

"I do love you and I am sorry." I told him.

"I love you too." He pressed a kiss to my forehead.

"So…did you have fun last night?" I inquired, trying to change the subject quickly.

"I was too worried." He shook his head.

"I'm sorry." I offered an apologetic smile.

"It's not your fault." He replied.

"Did you tell Leader Syphex about the possible threat? Maybe he can do something." I suggested.

"I doubt it." He scoffed.

"Really?" I queried.

"He seems rather preoccupied these days." He informed me.

"Huh." I replied.

During a few moments of awkward silence, I studied Keylan's face. He seemed troubled and somber, probably because of my harsh words. I knew apologizing would do little, so I decided to distract him in another way.

"Why don't we stop worrying about it and watch a holoprogram?" I suggested.

"Sure." He sighed in relief.

I could tell he wanted a break from the stress that politics brought. Although he was a strong and capable Commander, he seemed not to enjoy the world of politics. I racked my brain for any memories of him before the Reforming, trying to figure him out. Perhaps he truly wasn't cut out for politics; maybe he had joined the military before the Reforming for other reasons.

"Keylan." I chirped.

"Yes, angel?" He responded, half-distracted by the holoprojector.

"What was your name before the Reforming?" I interrogated.

I regretted my question as I sensed him tense up beside me.

"It's okay if you don't want to tell me, I was just curious." I shrugged, snuggling into him.

I wondered if he didn't want to share his name because he had done something bad before. Maybe I did know him, and I would remember his deeds as soon as he told me.

"No, it's okay," he returned, "my name was Mathac Dain."

I pushed away from him immediately. He stared at me with a confused expression as I scooted to the other side of the bed, away from him.

"You were Major Dain?" I gasped.

"Do you remember me?" His face paled.

"Yes..." I breathed, "I didn't...I didn't even realize you were him...that he is you...that you're...you."

He chuckled lightheartedly at my ramblings.

"What all do you remember?" He questioned.

"A lot." I chuckled.

"Tell me." He urged.

"You were always so nice...to everyone, regardless of what they did," I told him, "I remember you'd always listen to me unlike the others who just ignored me because I was a child. You would sneak me candy when my mom wasn't looking, and you would always help everyone."

"I'm glad your memories of me are so nice." He laughed.

"I remember more." I said.

He motioned for me to continue, relaxing back into the bed. I wonder if he would tense once more after I told him what else I knew or if he would be relieved.

"I remember you saving my mother's life." I confessed.

His face drained of all color again as he shifted uncomfortably.

"How did you go from that to someone known for angry outbursts and killing thousands in the Reforming?" I questioned.

"I told you what happened." He snapped.

I wanted to argue with him, to tell him that his pain was no reason to lash out at people. I didn't want to, though. I knew that what had happened had hurt him badly and I didn't want him to be upset. I crawled back over to him and crossed my legs while staring up at him lovingly.

"You're such an amazing person." I smiled.

I wanted to continue by urging him to let others see it, despite his painful past. Maybe another time I would, but not tonight.

"Did you ever think back then that you'd end up being with me?" I giggled.

"No," he chortled, "but I couldn't even imagine how beautiful of a woman you'd grow up to be."

"Aw shucks." I replied playfully.

"Now are we going to watch something or not?" He raised an eyebrow.

I nodded and snuggled into his chest, paying more attention to his strong heartbeat than the holoprogram. I found myself feeling quite fatigued as I relaxed next to him, and soon fell asleep in his arms. The next day continued as normal until after lunch, when we were informed by an officer that the Supreme Order Dignitaries would not be joining us for the afternoon meetings; we decided to continue with our meetings on the benefits of an alliance in the event of a war without them. I worried throughout meetings and dinner, making little conversation with Lorne.

As soon as I was ready for bed and out of sight, I hurried off to Keylan's rooms. No one had hinted at them missing the afternoon's meeting and he had not said anything to me about it either. I wondered if something was wrong, and he needed to leave me. I burst into his rooms to see his things thrown everywhere.

"Keylan?" I called him.

He stormed out into the sitting room, making me step back. His eyes were wild, and his face was red. His fists were clenched tightly, one of his hands holding a red lasersword.

"Is everything okay?" I squeaked.

He turned off the lasersword and threw it to the side.

"Go back to your rooms," he commanded, "I will see you tomorrow morning."

A lump rose in my throat as I nodded and turned to leave. I did not let the tears fall from my eyes until I was safe in my rooms. Feeling distraught, I called the only friend I had that knew about me and Keylan.

"What's wrong?" Joyriak asked as she entered my rooms. She rushed over to me, delicately drying my tears with her thumbs.

"I went to see Keylan and he just told me to leave." I sniffled.

"Is that it?" She chuckled, wrapping her arm around my shoulders, "sweetie, he's probably just stressed."

"Why?" My voice broke.

"They're nearing their deadline," she said, "you have less than 2 months to make an alliance."

"That doesn't negatively affect him." I retorted.

"But it negatively affects you and your kingdom," she argued, "he's probably worried about you…especially with the recent threats."

"He seemed really upset," I told her, "His room was wrecked and he had a lasersword in his hand when I came in."

"Are you sure he wasn't fighting someone in there?" She chortled.

"No…I think he was having a tantrum or something." I pulled my knees to my chest.

"Just talk to him tomorrow and sort everything out," she smiled reassuringly, "communication is very important in a relationship."

"Okay." I sniffed.

"Hey, it's going to be fine," she assured me, "I have no idea how it happened, but somehow you two are deeply in love. You'll work everything out."

Despite her soothing advice, her reassuring words, and her presence for the remainder of the night, I started to feel incredibly ill. The anxiety I had over what had happened and what was to happen made my stomach churn. My nervousness was less focused on losing Keylan and more focused on a possible situation. Since we had been romantically involved, he had had no real tantrums that I remembered. He was calm with me, not acting like everyone said he did.

"Joyriak?" I croaked as I woke up from my torrid sleep.

"Yeah?" She blinked awake.

"Can you help me to the bathroom? I feel ill." I said.

Despite her obvious reluctance to be awake, she popped up and assisted me. I retched into the toilet while Joyriak faithfully held up my hair as I expelled the day's food. As soon as I was finished, she helped me to sit against the wall and went to fetch me a glass of water. While I drank the water slowly, she cleaned my face with a wet cloth.

"What's wrong?" She inquired as she cleaned me up.

"I guess I'm just anxious." I chuckled shakily.

"About the situation with the Commander?" She asked, throwing the cloth into a laundry hamper.

I nodded weakly before taking the tiniest sip of water.

"I told you, everything's going to be fine," She stroked my hair comfortingly, "let me help you back to bed, okay? I'll inform your parents you'll be staying in your rooms for the day."

"No, I can go." I protested.

"You're ill, Aza, you need rest." She countered.

I groaned as she helped me to my feet and lead me back to bed. She led me through morning devotionals, prayers, and meditations before heading out to inform everyone I was ill. My sphoas did not come that day at the request of Joyriak, leaving the two of us to watch our favorite holoprograms in my room for a while.

"It's breakfast time, I'll go get you some food." Joyriak offered as the second holoprogram ended.

"No, I don't feel well enough to eat." I insisted.

"You need to eat, Aza." She scolded.

"I can't even look at food right now, Joyriak," I argued, "please, let's just rest and watch holoprograms."

Joyriak reluctantly agreed and joined me in bed once more. I drifted

in and out of sleep, often waking from a nightmare involving the

Supreme Order. As a result of this, I endeavored to stay awake as

long as I possibly could.

Throughout the day, my friend took good care of me. She fetched me

aa cold cloth when I got too warm, wrapped me in blankets when I

got too cold, and kept me distracted so I wouldn't worry too much. I

wished she would take a break and let someone else help me,

especially since she had barely slept last night, but I knew she would

be too stubborn.

"It's lunchtime now," she said, "I'm getting you food."

"Really, Joyriak, I'm not hungry." I insisted.

"You need to eat, or your anxiety will just get worse." She returned.

"Not too much, okay?" I said.

She nodded before hurrying out the door. Even though I wanted her

to take a break from looking after me, I missed her presence. There

was something comforting about having someone you trusted next to

you.

I smiled as I heard the doors slide open, cheerfully awaiting my best friend. However, the footsteps did not sound like hers at all. Hers were delicate, quick, and purposeful. These footsteps were heavy, slow, and deliberate. I frowned as the footsteps approached my bedroom.

"Keylan." I breathed as he appeared in my bedroom door.

He set the tray on the bench at the end of my bed and removed his helmet. His dark locks fell out it, framing his pale face perfectly somehow. He set the helmet beside the tray and hurried to my side, sitting on the bed next to me.

"What are you doing here?" I questioned.

"I caught Joyriak in the kitchens, she was quite upset," he explained, "I think she blamed me for making you ill. I told her that she needed a break and that I would bring your lunch to you….and apologize."

"And she agreed?" I scoffed, "that doesn't sound like her at all."

"She seemed exhausted." He informed me.

"Oh." I replied, feeling bad that I'd worked her to exhaustion.

"Azalyn, I'm so sorry if I made you feel badly last night, it wasn't my intention at all," he apologized, "during our meeting with Leader Syphex I heard something very troubling, and I was extremely upset."

"What did you hear?" I interrogated.

His apology did not sound much like him, which made me suspicious. I thought perhaps he was genuinely worried and was trying to make it up to me or he was unauthentic.

"I can't tell you right now." He responded somberly.

"Why not?" I pressed.

"Leader Syphex doesn't want us revealing anything," he answered, "but if it's any consolation, I want to tell you everything."

"I understand that you can't." I smiled reassuringly.

He smiled in response before moving to retrieve the tray. He set it between the two of us and we began to eat our lunch together.

"One day, I will be able to tell you anything I please." He stated.

"Why do you say that?" I queried.

"I'm going to be higher ranking one day and I'll be able to do as I please." He continued.

"You can't go any higher, unless you become Leader." I giggled.

He gave me a serious look and I realized he wasn't joking.

"Keylan, you'd have to kill him." I whispered.

"I know." He replied.

"Okay, stop being silly and get this tray off my bed." I laughed nervously.

He obeyed my order, and we avoided the topic for the rest of our time together. Instead, we watched holoprograms and talked about the meetings that day. He sent for dinner around the time everyone else was eating, then he stayed for the night. Although we didn't speak further on the subject, I was genuinely worried the entire time he was with me. Could he really be planning to kill the Leader? Did he seriously want to be Leader that badly? And if so, why? What was happening that he thought he needed to be higher ranking? Finally, what had Leader Syphex said that I couldn't know?

The next day I was able to calm my nerves enough to go to meetings. Everything went as normal, although I felt a bit paranoid. Keylan's words and demeanor the past couple days had been frightening me.

My fears were washed away that night as I spent it with him in his rooms. He acted just as he normally did, except for a few odd comments here and there. I could tell that whatever Leader Syphex had said was troubling him, but at least now he was back to normal.

"What do you think of the current government in Soturna?" Keylan suddenly questioned me.

"I think it works well," I answered, "there are some improvements to be made but I like the overall setup."

"So, you think well of the situation with the Royal Families and Senatorial Families?" He continued.

"Of course, don't you?" I returned.

"I do," he smiled, "I think you're absolutely right to think well of it."

I chuckled awkwardly, wondering where he was going with this.

"You're such a good ruler, Azalyn, such a good Cerulea," he complimented, "and you will make such a good Lumina."

"Thank you...but you're scaring me with all this." I chuckled nervously.

"I'm sorry," he chortled, "like I told you, I'm just troubled by what Leader Syphex said."

"I understand." I assured him.

"Let's just avoid the political talk for tonight, okay?" He suggested.

"Yeah." I agreed.

Unfortunately, after another long day of boring meetings, politics was all we could talk about. We were now halfway through the second month of the Supreme Order being here. That meant we only had a month and a half to make the alliance.

"We've been meeting almost every day for a month," I said as I entered his rooms, "why the hell haven't we gotten anywhere?"

"Leader Syphex is screwing everything up." He mumbled.

"He sent you here to make the alliance, why does he suddenly have an issue with everything?" I whined.

"He's changed." Keylan answered.

I gave him a questioning look as I joined him on the couch. He looked as troubled as he had the day he'd told me to leave. I placed my hand on his back comfortingly, hoping he wouldn't lash out again.

"You can fix this." I reassured him.

"I will fix this." He returned.

"I know," I smiled, "but let's not worry about it anymore tonight."

"What did you think of Lorne's opinions on the international view of the alliance?" He smirked.

"Poor kid really needs some more lessons in politics." I laughed.

"I might have to talk to Leader Syphex about his future position." Keylan mused.

"Oh, don't," I said, "he's sweet and his heart is in the right place."

"It doesn't matter if he's incompetent as a Senator." He argued.

I shrugged, knowing he was right. We continued to converse about the day's meetings as well as the subject of tomorrow's meetings. I discovered that we had different views on many things, which was new for us. Even when we did disagree, we were able to come to some sort of compromise. Tonight, there was a rift between us, finally frustrating us to the point that we fell asleep in silence.

Chapter Twenty-One: The Repair

The next morning, I snuck out before Keylan could awaken. As soon as I arrived the door to my rooms, I commanded one of the officers to call for Joyriak. With one more glance behind me to make sure Keylan had not followed, I slipped into my rooms. I readied myself for the day so the need for sphoas would be mitigated.

"Hey, are you sick again?" Joyriak asked as she entered my rooms.

"Nope, I'm just staying home for the day." I grinned.

"Why?" She questioned, joining me on the couch.

"I just need a day to myself." I replied.

"So, you're avoiding the Commander?" She raised an eyebrow.

I avoided her question, instead picking up the remote to the holoprojector.

"I thought you guys talked when he came here the other day." She continued.

"We did, but he's all stressed and weird about something Leader Syphex told him." I groaned.

"What did he tell him?" She pressed.

"No idea, he can't tell me." I confessed.

"So, it's the secret that's driving a wedge between the two of you." She pulled her knees into her chest.

"I guess…it seems like we're not getting along as well anymore." I told her.

She nodded slowly, studying my face diligently.

"I know this relationship is new and…different," I sighed, "but I really do love him, and I want to commit to him and make this work."

"I know. Maybe you two should do something fun together," she suggested, "it'll take your minds off of all this political stuff and hopefully strengthen your relationship."

"Yes! And I'll stay away from him today. Absence always makes our heart grow…" I stopped to laugh after realizing my mistake, "*hearts* grow fonder."

"So, I should tell the sphoas they have the day off and have the chalis bring your meals here for today?" She inquired.

"Yep…we'll spend the day binge-watching holoprograms and eating." I laughed.

"Sounds good to me!" She replied enthusiastically.

After our usual morning ritual, Joyriak made the proper

arrangements for the day. My sphoas would leave us be and the

chalis would only come in to bring us our meals. As soon as my

halcyns arrived, she told them not to let Keylan see me should he ask

to.

As we suspected, Keylan came looking for me during lunch. He

seemed upset after being refused, but I knew I would remedy the

situation the next day. Today, I was going to focus on relaxing with

my friend.

I decided to spend the next day at home as well. After my usual

morning routine and breakfast in bed, I sent Joyriak to Keylan's

rooms. There, she was to tell one of his officers to retrieve him and

bring him to the castle's gym.

"Hey," Joyriak called as she returned to my rooms, "ready to go?"

I hopped up from the couch and nodded excitedly. We hurried

through the halls toward the gym, where Joyriak left me alone. As

soon as she was gone, I set to work unlocking the Supreme Order's

case on the wall. To my surprise, it had been left unlocked. I

retrieved the training lasersword Keylan had given me and began to

practice what he had shown me so far.

"What are you doing?" Keylan questioned as he entered the gym.

"Close the blockers." I demanded

He frowned as he closed the door behind him. With a confused expression plastered on his face, he pushed the button to lower the privacy shields over the glass walls, effectively blocking us from the view of curious onlookers. As he stepped towards me, I retrieved his lasersword and threw it to him, careful not to turn it on as I did so.

"What's going on?" He queried, turning his lasersword on as he caught it.

"Fight me." I smirked.

He advanced, quickly swinging the lasersword at me. I blocked it, my arms aching as a result of the impact. He continued on the offensive as I blocked him as well as I could. Eventually he bested me, kicking the lasersword out of my hand. I stared at him with wide eyes as he approached me. He backed me up to the corner of the gym where the mats were stacked. He turned off his lasersword and threw it across the room before tackling me.

"Hey!" I whined.

"Are you going to tell me what all this is about?" He smirked.

"We're just…struggling with this political stuff," I confessed, "Joyriak suggested that maybe we should just do something fun to take our minds off of it."

"I would have picked another trip to an island, but I guess this is fine." He chuckled, leaning back on his heels.

I pushed myself up and playfully hit his chest. He laughed in response before frowning in thought.

"I want you to know that I am sorry I can't tell you everything," he said, "I don't want to keep secrets from you like this."

"I know...and I understand," I replied, "your job is important, and I know you need to keep this secret from me for it."

"I don't want it to affect our relationship," he continued, "so I'll try to keep work separate from our relationship."

"We can handle it." I smiled.

He grinned in response and pulled me closer to him. I snuggled into his chest, enjoying the peaceful moment.

"I really think I should become Supreme Leader," he whispered, "then everything would work out for us."

"It would be nice to not have to hide." I jested.

"It's settled then." He returned.

"What? No!" I pushed off of him, "I'm joking Keylan, you can't do that."

He nodded and took a deep breath, running his hands through his hair.

"I know…I'm loyal to Syphex." He sighed.

I'd never heard him call the Leader by only his name. In fact, I hadn't heard anyone refer to him by only his name. It was always 'Leader' or 'Leader Syphex'.

"So, what did you think of my technique?" I changed the subject.

"A few mistakes but otherwise good." He commented.

"Show me what to do." I stood.

He stood to join me and began to show me what mistakes I had done. Once I had properly corrected my mistakes, he showed me a new move. By lunchtime, I had practically perfected the move.

"Lunch in your rooms?" I panted; my energy drained from training.

"I'll have my officers fetch it for us." He agreed, taking my lasersword from me.

After a calm lunch, we were right back in the gym to train. If anyone was suspicious of us, they had no time to inquire after us. Other than the 30 minutes it took us to eat lunch, we were out of our rooms. Even though the lasersword training was tiring, I felt completely rejuvenated after our day together.

Following a private dinner, we cuddled under the covers of Keylan's bed and fell asleep almost instantly. It took everything in me to leave him and his warm bed the next morning, but I knew I had to return to meetings sometime. If I didn't, we would definitely get caught.

The day went as normal, except for Keylan calling me after dinner to continue our lasersword training. According to him, I was doing very well, and I needed to continue to train every day. It was probably just an excuse for us to be together doing something fun, but I didn't mind; I loved Keylan and I loved lasersword training.

"You have to meet me at the gym tomorrow… right after dinner." Keylan instructed as we strolled out of the gym.

"On a Sunday?" I inquired.

"There's no law against exercising on Sunday." He returned.

"There is a law against working on Sunday, though." I argued.

"You consider lasersword training a job?" He smirked.

"No, but…" I started.

"If you don't want to see me, that's fine." He interrupted; his tone playful.

"You're so annoying," I rolled my eyes, "I'll be there."

"Awesome." He smirked, kissing my forehead.

I hurried to the gym as soon as I was changed out of my day clothes. The day had gone as most Sundays did, filled only with church, meals, and family time. I didn't really want to train after our big Sunday dinner, but I knew Keylan would be upset if I didn't show up.

Apparently, he had expected me to show up much later, as he was already in the gym doing his own training when I arrived. The blockers weren't down, so I could watch him easily from where I was standing in the hall. His arm muscles, visible as a result of the black tank top he was wearing, rippled with each move he made. He swung the lasersword gracefully about the room, moving more skillfully than he did when mock-fighting me.

I studied each move he made, making mental notes as I did so. It was obvious to me now why everyone called him the greatest lasersword fighter and I felt that, as his girlfriend, I needed to match him. Then again, he had much more practice than I did.

As he finished his own training, he noticed me standing outside and motioned for me to join him. I blushed in embarrassment as I scurried inside the gym, closing the blockers behind me. He smirked as he watched me nervously prepare for training. His eyes, which never looked away from me, had a mischievous gleam as he grabbed a drink of water. I stumbled around, trying to hide my embarrassment from him.

"Ready to start?" he asked, twirling both of our laserswords in his hands.

I nodded sheepishly, and he threw me my lasersword. I fumbled as I caught it, still preoccupied with my recent embarrassment. After teaching me a few new moves, we moved onto our mock fighting. Of course, he won again, to my chagrin.

"Can you please teach me how to, like, win?" I asked as I pushed myself back onto my feet.

"Just practice." He grinned.

I groaned and rolled my eyes at him. Turning the lasersword off and setting it down, I stepped over to my water bottle and collapsed next to it. Keylan laughed at me as I took a huge drink of water.

"How about I teach you some partner choreography?" he proposed.

I sat up straight and gave him a questioning look.

"There's choreography in lasersword fighting?" I inquired.

"Sometimes." He shrugged.

"I guess I'll try it." I sighed as I stood up.

Despite him trying his best to teach me the choreography, I still could not do it. I wondered if the discord between us was causing us to not work as well as we usually did. Perhaps we should talk about the weirdness between us resulting from the secret he kept from me instead of avoiding it by doing lasersword training all the time.

"All right, let's maybe try it with guns?" he suggested.

"Guns?" I questioned.

"Yeah." He replied, extinguishing his lasersword.

"Why do you guys even have choreography for fighting?" I pressed, "it seems rather useless for a battle."

"It's actually quite helpful, which you would know if you'd ever actually been in a war." He snapped.

I extinguished my lasersword and threw the hilt down at his feet before stomping towards the door. Keylan's heavy footsteps sounded quickly behind me.

"Hey, hey, hey, wait," he said, grabbing me in his arms, "I'm sorry, I didn't mean for it to sound like that."

"Like what? Condescending?" I mumbled.

"Yes," he chuckled, "now can we just get back to training?"

"Fine." I growled, pushing out of his grasp.

When we were thoroughly exhausted from gun training, we trudged back to his rooms. I collapsed into his bed, unable to stand a moment longer. I fell asleep knowing the next day would be rough for both of us.

Somehow the two of us managed to stay awake and alert during the day's meetings. I half-expected Keylan to let me have a break that night, but this expectation was not met. He did, however, allow us to include a bit of boxing and gun training with our regular lasersword training. After failing miserably in comparison to his incredibleness with a lasersword, this was a welcome change.

"Ow! Jeez!" Keylan remarked as I kicked the strike shield once more.

"I told you I have strong legs," I smirked, "dancer, remember?"

"Yeah, let's maybe move on." He groaned.

I beamed at this, knowing that I had beaten him in at least one thing. He seemed to be better than me at everything, so I liked winning at something, even though he seemed bothered by it.

"Unfortunately for you, lasersword fighting and shooting require more arm strength," he handed me my lasersword, "so that's what we need to really focus on."

"You're just mad I'm a better kickboxer than you." I teased.

"But I'm still better with a lasersword." He smirked.

"Prove it." I challenged, picking up my lasersword.

He ignited his lasersword and charged towards me, leaving me just enough time to duck out of the way. I fought him off as well as I could, my heart beating wildly in my chest. The fight ended with him pushing me back onto one of the mats, the blade of his lasersword just centimeters from my neck.

"Okay, you win." I chuckled nervously.

"If you can hold your own against me, you'll be able to beat everyone else." He commented, extinguishing his lasersword.

"Arrogant much?" I joked, brushing myself off as I stood up.

"Not arrogant, just confident." He smirked.

Chapter Twenty-Two: The Division

"I think that the Supreme Order should continue to progress as it has the past few years," Senator Varros said, "with a separate government for each kingdom."

"Are you suggesting that the kingdoms of Soturna secede from the Supreme Order?" Hanew scoffed.

"Not necessarily, I just think it is best if each kingdom creates their own distinct government, while still keeping the rules of the Supreme Order." Senator Varros answered.

"Senator, the Supreme Order has brought peace and prosperity to this nation," I argued, "Soturna has fallen to ruin in the past few years as a result of these kingdoms trying to gain independence from the Supreme Order. We need to return to how it was before if we wish to live in peace again."

"I think the Supreme Order is the reason we're in this mess in the first place." Senatress Varros spoke up.

"If that is how the Senatorial Family feels about the Supreme Order, I think it's best we leave these meetings," Keylan stood, "Lumin, Lumina, if you'd be so kind as to send our dinners to our rooms."

The faces of my parents went pale as the eyes of the Senatorial Family widened. My father managed a nod as the Supreme Order Dignitaries marched out of the room. Captain Plutan looked as if she wanted to stay and make peace but followed her superior out of the room.

"If you'll excuse me." I said as soon as all the Supreme Order Dignitaries had left.

I stood and stormed out of the room, making sure to use my body language to let the Senatorial Family know how displeased I was. I knew I shouldn't be so obviously rude to them, especially when we were trying to make an alliance with them, but I also knew they could ruin everything for both our families.

"Aza!" Lorne called, running out of the meeting room after me.

"What, Lorne?" I snarled, whipping around quickly.

He stepped back, as if he were taken aback by my response.

"Where are you going?" he questioned.

"I don't think that's any of your business, honestly." I folded my arms over my chest.

"Did I do something? Why haven't you been hanging out with me lately?" he interrogated.

"I've been busy." I retorted.

"Are you mad at me?" he pressed.

"I have every right to be, considering your family openly insulted the Supreme Order just now," I spat, "you're putting our alliance with the Supreme Order in jeopardy. You're putting our kingdom and our lives in danger. Think about that."

Without another word, I turned on my heel and sped off towards Keylan's rooms. If there was anyone who could calm the Commander of the Supreme Order down, it was me; that meant it was my responsibility to talk to him.

"Hey Keylan?" I called as I entered his seemingly vacant rooms, "babe?"

He came storming out of his bedroom with disheveled hair, clenched fists, and no shirt.

"Are you...um, are you okay?" I stammered, studying his form. I'd never noticed before that he had a couple of scars on his body. They were small, barely noticeable, but still there. I wondered what he'd gotten them from.

"The Senatorial Family is openly insulting us in a meeting, I would say I'm not great." He snapped.

"Yeah, I figured," I sighed, "look, I know they're not the most politically savvy people or anything, but for my kingdom's sake, just…compromise."

He studied my face for a moment, before taking a deep breath and unclenching his fists.

"The Supreme Order really has gone to hell," Keylan ran his hands through his hair, "we need to get it back to the way it was. That's why Canada and the Rogues are attacking all of a sudden…we've changed and we're weak."

"I agree with you," I replied, placing a comforting hand on his shoulder, "and we'll get it back to the way it was."

"If it came down to it," he turned to face me, "would you stand with me and rule Soturna with me?"

"Of course," I frowned, "but we don't need to do anything drastic yet."

He nodded in agreement as he tenderly stroked my hair. He stared lovingly down at me, making me feel calm and gleeful.

"Are you staying with me for the rest of the night?" he queried.

"If you want me to." I smiled.

"You know I do." He chuckled.

I decided not to ask him if we were going to train tonight. I was still sore from the past few nights of training, and I didn't want to remind him about it. Thankfully, his preoccupation with the issues during the meetings took precedence.

The next day's meetings were tense but civil, which was good enough for me. Even though I knew it was selfish, all I really cared about at these meetings was that my kingdom made alliances both with the Supreme Order and the kingdom of Waskaura. If nothing else, Keylan was right about one thing: we were seeing much more attacks from both the Canadians and the Rogues.

After lunch, we began to revisit the terms of the alliance, which we had discussed at the beginning of our meetings together. I had to stop myself from rolling my eyes as we conversed about things we had talked about weeks ago; I didn't see why we had to review them once more.

"I don't know that a mutual exchange of resources would be equal." Hanew said.

"Why do you think that General?" My mother inquired.

"The Supreme Order is higher up than both the Asphoamist and Waskaura kingdoms." he responded.

"We're not suggesting that you give us more," my father explained, "just that we provide each other the resources we need as we need them."

"We won't deplete the Supreme Order's resources, General." I flashed a smile at him.

He melted immediately and I knew that my tactic had worked, even though Keylan wouldn't appreciate it.

"I think we all agree on the terms, then?" Senator Varros asked.

Everyone nodded in agreement, looking at the others to see if they were doing the same. I smiled at the sight.

"It seems the terms of the alliance are finalized," my father announced, "now, are there any more requests before dinner?"

Silence followed my father's question.

"Very well, shall we?" My father stood.

We all shuffled off to the dining hall, where we ate dinner quietly. I could sense tension between all of our families, but I comforted myself with the thought that at least we had made progress with the alliance. I was starting to worry that alliances might never be formed, since we were approaching the end of our second to last month together.

Directly after I had changed into my nightclothes, I scurried off to Keylan's rooms. He was sitting on the couch reading a book when I arrived, seeming much more relaxed than he had been the past few days. I smiled at the peaceful sight.

"Hey." He greeted me, placing the book on the coffee table.

"Hey." I replied.

I took my place next to him, glancing over at the book as I did so.

"Plato's *Republic*?" I questioned.

"I thought it was worth re-reading, especially around this time." He shrugged.

"Thank you for being civil with the Senatorial Family today." I smiled.

"Only for you." He sighed, flashing me a playful grin.

"We just need to ally everyone and then everything will be just as it was." I assured him.

"Will it?" He returned.

"We'll make it be the way it was." I said confidently.

"I think we need to do much more than just ally everyone." He argued.

"I think allying everyone is the first step," I contradicted, "that way we can work together to return peace to Soturna."

He beamed and nodded. His dark eyes studied my face lovingly, making me blush.

"What would we do if we ruled the nation?" He queried.

"What do you mean?" I chuckled.

"If we changed the way things are," he said, "if the two of us became the Leaders of the nation."

"Can I be an empress?" I giggled.

"If you want." He chortled.

"Well, as Empress of Soturna," I laughed, sitting up straighter, "I would conquer the Rogue Islands and Canada. I would join them to the nation and restore peace to everyone."

"And how would you go about restoring peace?" He leaned back on the couch.

"We'd all talk…have meetings and such," I explained, "and we'd all agree on how the nation should be run. That way everyone has a say and is happy with the nation."

"So, you'd give the smaller kingdoms you ruled over… power?" He inquired.

"Yes, I think it would work best." I replied.

"And what makes you think these people would know how to properly rule a nation?" He interrogated.

"I didn't say I think that…I would just take their thoughts into account, so they felt heard." I responded.

"If I'm ever the Leader of Soturna," he took my hands in his, "I promise that I will conquer Canada for you and gift it to you. It will be your kingdom."

"What about Asphoamist?" I frowned.

"Your sister can rule it. That way you both can have your own kingdoms." He smiled.

I grinned happily.

"I wish that could happen." I chuckled.

"It will." He smoothed a curl behind my ear tenderly.

"Don't be silly." I scolded.

"Just wait." He whispered, pulling me onto his lap.

I let the subject go for the night, hoping he seriously wasn't considering doing something rash. If he tried to overthrow Leader Syphex, he'd certainly be imprisoned, if not killed.

"Wanna watch something?" I cheerfully suggested, retrieving the remote to the holoprojector.

"Sure." He beamed.

I flipped through the channels, searching for anything not related to politics. He'd been talking an awful lot about how he would rule Soturna lately and I didn't want him to think too much about it. If he did, he might seriously do the things he was talking about.

Thankfully, political conversation was completely avoided through the night. In the morning, I simply pressed a kiss to his forehead before sneaking back to my rooms. I could be a bit more careless now that Joyriak knew, but I still snuck back early every morning I stayed in his rooms.

As soon as I was dressed and ready for the day, I hurried off to breakfast. I dreaded talking politics, fearing it would influence Keylan too much, but I knew it must be done. It was especially important that we continue talking politics now that we were so close to forming alliances.

"Hey there, Aza." Lorne greeted me cheerfully.

Although his tone was jovial, I could tell he was still nervous about talking to me. Our last interaction had been less than friendly, and it wasn't like we had been hanging out a lot before that conversation. Honestly, our friendship had been very strained since the ball.

"Hey." I smiled.

"How are you?" He chirped.

"Fine...I guess. You?" I returned.

"I feel great." He informed me.

"Did Joyriak bring you an extra coffee?" I joked.

"Nope, I just have a great feeling about today." He answered.

"Okay." I chuckled.

Breakfast was uneventful, as usual. Except for the fidgeting of Senator and Senatress Varros, nothing gave me any clue of what was to happen at the end of breakfast.

"Lumin, we were wondering if we might have five days of private meetings with you and the Lumina." Senatress Varros spoke up.

I frowned in confusion. Five days was a lot, and an oddly specific number of days. Why would the Senatorial Family want five days of private meetings with my parents? I looked over at Lorne, who seemed just as confused as I was, then at Keylan. He stared back at me, as if waiting to see if I knew anything about the inquiry.

"I think that will be all right." My father looked over at the Supreme Order Dignitaries for approval.

I watched as Keylan nodded slightly, giving his approval. The General, Captain, and Lieutenant shared subtle, confused expressions. It was painfully obvious that no one except for the Senator and Senatress knew what was going on. I just hoped it was nothing bad since we were so close to making alliances with both the Supreme Order and Waskaura.

As soon as breakfast was finished, I dodged Lorne and hurried off to Keylan's rooms. It probably would have been a better idea to just ask Lorne what was going on, but I would rather ask Keylan.

"Hey, what's going on?" I asked as I entered his rooms.

Keylan was tapping rapidly on his holopad, his brows furrowed in thought. I sat on the couch, waiting for him to acknowledge me.

"That's what I'm trying to figure out," He replied, "I'm contacting Leader Syphex about the situation."

"You mean with the Senator and Senatress scheduling private meetings?" I clarified.

He nodded in response.

"I can try to talk to Lorne, but I don't think he knows anything." I shrugged.

"No…just stay away from him for now," he said, "we'll meet with Leader Syphex today and get everything figured out."

"So, what am I supposed to do?" I pouted.

He put his holopad down and crossed over to me. He bent down to gently kiss the top of my head.

"Just call your friends and relax for the day." He smiled.

"Are you sure?" I asked.

"You need a break from all this." He chuckled.

"Okay." I relented.

I stood reluctantly from the couch.

"Try not to worry too much, my princess." He urged.

"I'll try." I sighed.

"I'll miss you." He admitted, pulling me into an embrace.

"I'll miss you too." I whispered.

With a kiss on the lips and then on the forehead, Keylan sent me on my way. I trudged back to my own rooms, dreading the day now. I called Joyriak to my rooms first, wanting to speak with her about recent events; she was the only one who could know the entire story.

"Day off?" She questioned as she entered my rooms.

"Yep…the Senator and Senatress requested five days of private meetings with my parents." I informed me.

"Why aren't you and Lorne going?" She interrogated.

"No idea." I shrugged.

"Does the Commander know anything?" She pressed.

"None of the Supreme Order Dignitaries knew anything." I told her.

"Did Lorne?" She asked.

"He seemed just as clueless as me." I sighed.

"Huh. I wonder what's going on." She mused.

"Keylan's scheduling meetings with the Leader to figure things out." I said.

"You don't think they'll leave, do you?" She queried.

"I hope Keylan won't let them." I responded.

"Yeah, that would be bad for the alliance." She chuckled.

I twisted my sheets between my fingers, thinking about what could be done. I needed to figure out what was going on, and right now there was no way for me to figure it out. My parents were meeting with Senator and Senatress, the Supreme Order Dignitaries would be in meetings with Leader Syphex by now, and Keylan had warned me to stay away from Lorne.

"Hey, can you maybe spend the day with Lorne?" I asked, "I call the girls and we'll go dance…maybe you can find something out."

"I'm on it." She grinned, standing.

"Thanks, you're the best." I smiled, rising to embrace her.

"I know it." She joked.

As soon as she was off on her mission, I called my other alysseas to my room. We did as I told Joyriak we'd do and went straight to the dance studio. We broke briefly for lunch, which the chalis brought us, but otherwise did not stop until I was pulled away for dinner.

While I was getting ready for dinner, Wupera informed me that Joyriak had requested to see me later tonight. I responded by telling her to call Joyriak to my rooms as soon as I returned from dinner. I needed to talk to her as soon as possible, but I also wanted to spend the night with Keylan. I could get valuable information from both of them tonight.

The topic of meetings was expertly avoided by all at dinner. Even so, it was obvious that the Supreme Order Dignitaries felt a bit peeved about the private meetings my parents were having with Lorne's parents. I wondered if they suspected a plot against the Supreme Order or something like that.

As soon as the awkward dinner was over, I hurried off to my rooms to see Joyriak. I was anxious to hear any news she might have for me.

"What's up?" I inquired as I entered my rooms.

"Lorne told me all he knows is that his parents want him to talk to you a lot," she explained, "and that he is to be on his best behavior, especially around you."

"That probably means they want our kingdoms to form an alliance!" I exclaimed happily.

"You need to get dressed for bed and get to Keylan's rooms as soon as possible." She whispered anxiously.

"Why?" I questioned.

"I've heard whispers…of what was said in today's meetings…just rumors I think." She replied.

"Call my sphoas and I'll go immediately." I nodded.

She bowed out of my rooms to retrieve my sphoas. I tried to keep myself from getting too anxious as they prepared me for bed. As soon as they were out of sight, I scurried off to Keylan's rooms. He was relaxing on the couch watching a holoprogram when I arrived.

"I don't know what rumors are going around right now," I announced, "but I don't really care as long as you tell me what is going on."

He chuckled and motioned for me to sit next to him. I obeyed him and slung my legs over his lap, awaiting an explanation.

"We still aren't sure what the Senator and Senatress are doing, but we have suspicions," he explained, "regardless, we won't be leaving anytime soon. I promise to tell you if anything changes."

"But everything stays the same for now?" I clarified.

"Yes, little dove." He beamed.

"I sent Joyriak off to spend the day with Lorne," I confessed, "she said his parents told him to be extra nice to me and to make sure to spend a lot of time with me."

"All right, that narrows things down." He frowned.

"You think they're going to try to make an alliance with my kingdom?" I inquired.

"It's highly likely." He shrugged.

"And if they are? What will happen?" I interrogated.

"I'll have to talk with Leader Syphex, but you know I'm on your side," he replied, "I'll do everything I can to ally the Supreme Order with your kingdom."

"I appreciate it." I snuggled into his chest.

I spent the rest of the night thinking of ways I could help Keylan form an alliance with my kingdom. I was glad he stayed up so late since the idea came to me well after midnight.

"Keylan." I said.

"Huh?" He responded.

"Can I spend the day with Lorne tomorrow? I might be able to get some more information." I said.

"Aza, I told you I don't want you around him right now," he scolded, "just send Joyriak to him again."

"He might tell me more because I'm the Cerulea," I argued, "plus, I'll get all the information first-hand."

He scrunched his face up as he considered my words.

"If you feel unsafe or uncomfortable or unsettled in any way…" he replied, "you leave him and come straight to me. If I'm busy, go to Joyriak or one of the officers."

"I will," I agreed, "now I'm going to sleep."

"Okay, goodnight." He chuckled.

With that, I fell into a deep asleep.

Chapter Twenty-Three: The Agreements

As soon as breakfast was over the next day, I joined Lorne in the dance studio, per his request. He seemed very excited to spend time with me, probably because of his parents' instructions.

"What do you want to do?" I asked as I entered the dance studio in my dance clothes.

"Maybe we could sing again? Everyone loved it when we sang at the ball." He suggested.

"You perform for me first." I grinned, sitting cross-legged on the floor in front of him.

"Fine." He stuck his tongue out at me.

I watched him politely as he performed; I did enjoy listening to him, but I was more grateful that we were killing a bit of time. After we performed a few songs for each other, we took lunch privately in his rooms. He chattered excitedly, seeming almost flirtatious in his conversation. I hoped he was just thankful for my company.

"Do you want to go to the barns now?" Lorne asked as we finished lunch.

"Sure!" I answered, excited to see his fun side once more.

It was very annoying to be stuffed inside the castle with him, especially since he seemed ill at ease when he was inside. As I suspected, Lorne became more comfortable and fun around me as soon as we got outside. After a couple hours of interacting with the animals, Lorne and I made our way back to the castle.

Wanting to get some information from him so I'd have something to report, I suggested we go to the balcony at the top of the castle. One could get a glorious view from there and it would be especially pretty during the sunset. Fortunately, Lorne was more than happy to accompany me to the tower's balcony.

"It's so beautiful." Lorne sighed happily.

"Isn't it?" I replied.

"I've really enjoyed my time here with you, Aza." Lorne smiled.

"Why are you saying this? Are you leaving soon?" I inquired.

I wondered if maybe my assumptions had been wrong. Perhaps they weren't going to make an alliance and they were going to leave, but they wanted Lorne and I to remain friendly. Or perhaps they were going to make an alliance and Lorne was sad that he'd be ripped away from me so soon. But that couldn't be it…if they were going to make an alliance, they'd be here for at least another month for announcements and parties.

"No, no," he chuckled, "I just…I thought you should know how much I appreciate you."

"I appreciate you as well, Lorne," I grinned, "you're a good friend and I'm confident our kingdoms will be allied for many years."

I included the last sentence as a test for him. I wondered if he knew anything that was going on and had half a mind to ask him but thought better of it.

"I hope so." He smiled, brushing his hand against mine.

I merely smiled and moved my hand away before staring out at the kingdom below us, enjoying the cool breeze flowing through my hair.

"We should go." I said as he moved closer to me.

"Yeah." He sighed.

"I'll see you at dinner." I called back to him as I hurried back inside.

I groaned as I entered my rooms; I had barely gotten any information from Lorne the entire day. Keylan was going to be livid when he found out that I'd wasted my time with the boy.

Trying not to think about this, I readied myself for dinner and then hurried off to the dining hall. Once again, conversation was stiff and awkward. Lorne talked to me a bit more than usual, but that did not lift the uneasy feeling at the table.

Following the stifling dinner and a quick preparation for bed by my sphoas, I hurried off to Keylan's rooms. I was dreading telling him that I lacked any useful information, but I was also anxious to see if he had found out anything. I could guess well enough what was going to happen, but I wanted everything confirmed.

"What did you find out?" He asked as I entered his rooms.

Keylan stood stiffly in the dimly lit room, looking rather intimidating.

"He just said he enjoyed spending time with me and that he hopes our kingdoms will be allied for many years." I confessed.

He groaned in response to my answer.

"I'm sorry…he really didn't say anything else." I apologized.

"Don't worry about it, it's not your job anyways," he sighed, "but we did have meetings with Leader Syphex again today."

"And?" I pressed.

"We've all decided that it's very likely that your two kingdoms will be forming an alliance very soon." He answered.

"I agree…but what will happen?" I queried, "With Asphoamist and the Supreme Order?" I queried.

"I don't know yet," he replied, "but I promise I'll tell you as soon as I know."

"I know you will," I smiled, "but let's not talk about it anymore tonight."

I was utterly exhausted from the day; faking politeness around Lorne was draining. Besides, I'd been wasting extra energy worrying about what was going on. Lorne's sealed lips weren't really helping my anxiety, either.

"What would you like to do, my princess?" He grinned.

"I want…to go to sleep." I groaned.

"So early?" He chortled.

"Yes." I responded with a yawn.

"You sleep more than anyone I know." He chuckled.

"It's not my fault I'm surrounded my workaholics." I retorted.

"Maybe if you were a workaholic you'd be finished with levels by now." He teased.

"Yeah, I'd rather sleep twelve hours a day." I replied.

"Fair enough." He shrugged.

With that, I trudged off towards his bed, with him on my heels. I snuggled beneath the warm sheets as Keylan got dressed for bed. As he sat beside me, I moved closer to steal the warmth radiating off his body.

"I know you're tired, but I do need you to promise me something." Keylan said.

"What?" I muttered.

"I need you to promise me that you'll come here tomorrow, after church," he continued, "your parents will be meeting with the Senator and Senatress still so you shouldn't run in to any problems."

"Okay." I murmured before falling asleep.

As I had told Keylan I would, I hurried to his rooms straight after church and my family lunch. Thankfully, everyone was quite busy today, so we were left unbothered.

"So, what do you want?" I inquired as I strolled into his rooms and plopped down onto his couch.

"I have a proposal for you." He responded.

My eyes widened at his declaration.

"A what?" I stammered.

"Not that kind of proposal." He chuckled, kneeling in front of my legs.

"Well, what is your proposal?" I questioned.

"I think we should take another vacation, to get away from this mess." He announced.

"When? Where?" I interrogated.

"Tuesday…to Island 37." He answered.

"No…no, no, no, no, no." I scooted away from him and tucked my legs underneath me.

"I thought you'd say that." He sighed, joining me on the couch.

"Island 37 is banned!" I exclaimed.

"Not to the Supremes." He argued.

"Well, then you can go by yourself." I said.

"I said *we're* taking a vacation, not *I'm* taking a vacation." He retorted.

"I'm not a Supreme, Keylan." I folded my arms over my chest.

"Someday you will be." He smirked.

"How so?" I returned.

"By marriage." He grinned.

"That's a long way off and you know it." I countered.

He laughed and brushed a strand of hair out of my face.

"Well, how are you going to convince my parents to let you take me there?" I asked.

"We won't tell them which island we're going to." He replied.

"Are you suggesting we lie to my parents?" I scoffed.

"I didn't say we were going to lie…we'll just hide information from them." He responded.

"So, we'll just tell them we're going to an island?" I clarified.

He nodded, obviously proud of his plan.

"Fine, but if they ask where we're going, neither of us are going to lie." I asserted.

"As you wish." He sighed.

The next morning at breakfast, Keylan decided to make his move. I wanted him to ask at another time, but he'd convinced me this was the only time he could ask my parents. I had relented but was still worried about what everyone would think.

"Lumin, Lumina, I was wondering if I could take the Cerulea on another trip?" Keylan asked, "it might be good for her to take another political trip...especially since she is not doing anything right now."

I silently prayed that they would not ask where we were going.

"I think that would be all right...if she approves." My father responded.

"I'd be delighted to go." I beamed.

"It's settled then...when will you be going, Commander?" My mother returned.

"Tomorrow, Lumina." He replied.

My parents nodded in understanding. I thanked God that they'd not

asked where we were going as I tried to gauge everyone else's

reactions. The Supreme Order Dignitaries seemed unbothered,

except for Hanew, who seemed suspicious as usual. The Senator and

Senatress seemed a bit miffed, while Lorne appeared to be thinking

hard about something.

"Hey." Lorne grabbed my arm as we exited the dining hall.

"Yeah?" I answered.

"Can I come with you?" He inquired.

"To…to my rooms?" I stuttered.

"No, uh, on the vacation with the Commander tomorrow." He

corrected.

"Lorne, I'm sorry, but," I stammered, "I don't think the Commander

would…um…appreciate that."

"Oh, yeah, I understand." He replied.

"I'm sorry…he's kind of strict on this stuff, they all are," I

apologized, "maybe next time he'll invite you too, though? He just

doesn't know you that well yet."

"Maybe," he shrugged, "I'll see you around."

"Yeah, see you." I smiled.

He gave me a half-smile before walking away. I felt bad for the poor kid, but I really didn't want to even entertain the idea of him accompanying us. This was the only day Keylan and I had to be alone without worrying about anyone else. I was not giving it up just to make him feel better.

As soon as I returned to my rooms, I called Joyriak and told her of the trip Keylan and I would be taking. She immediately began to pack my bags per my instructions as I hurried off to Keylan to plan the trip with him.

"So, what's it like?" I questioned as I looked over what Keylan was packing.

"What? Island 37?" He returned.

"Yeah." I plopped down onto his bed.

"Gorgeous," he grinned, "the water is clear and blue and it's completely uninhabited."

"I thought you guys used it as a training center for the officers and rangers and stuff." I said.

"We used to…the overwater bungalows are still there from their training actually," he explained, "but we cleared it out and sent them all to Island 5."

"Is there a reason?" I inquired, twisting the fabric of the sheets between my fingers distractedly.

"Well, this happened long before you were even born," he chuckled, "but the French owned the set of islands we claimed, including Island 37, and then abandoned them. When we conquered them during the Reforming there were some issues. We had to move the Supremes to another island which was already owened by Soturna to prevent war."

"But you eventually won the islands…why didn't you just move the training centers back?" I pressed.

"It was just easier to leave them there." He shrugged.

"So now the Supreme Order just uses it as a vacation place or what?" I queried.

"We use it to hide weapons." He replied, giving me a serious look.

"You're taking me to an island filled with weapons?!" I exclaimed.

"Hush!" He scolded, "someone's going to hear you."

"I'm going to die. You're leading me to my death." I collapsed back on the bed.

"It's perfectly safe, little dove, I promise you." He assured me.

"If we die, I'm going to kill you." I informed him.

"Okay." He chortled.

"So, is that why the 85 Supreme Islands are prohibited?" I interrogated, "Because they hold weapons?"

"Some of them." He shrugged.

"Will I be able to visit all 85 one day?" I asked.

"Let's just start with one, okay?" He chuckled.

"Fine." I pouted.

After a couple minutes of silence spent looking up at the ceiling, I sat back up to face Keylan. He was busy packing, his face focused yet peaceful. I smiled at the sight of him carefully packing everything for tomorrow.

"Oh, by the way, Lorne stopped me on the way back from breakfast." I informed him, wanting to break the awkward silence. His head snapped up as he gave me his full attention.

"And?" He pressed.

"He asked to go with us tomorrow." I giggled.

"What did you tell him?" He sat on the bed next to me and grabbed my hands tightly.

"I told him maybe you'd invite him next time." I smirked.

Keylan scoffed and stood back up to restart his packing.

"Yeah, that's what I thought." I laughed.

Once Keylan was finished, he set his bags in the living room. I waited patiently for him in the bedroom, completely occupied with twisting the sheets between my fingers.

"Are you eating lunch here? I need to order." He said.

"Nope, I'm gonna head back to my rooms to talk with Joyriak about tomorrow." I stood.

"You two are eating alone?" He queried.

"Yeah…why?" I returned.

"Just making sure." He replied.

"Okay, well I'm gonna head out." I frowned.

I stopped as I came to the main doorway of his rooms and turned to look at him.

"Oh, by the way," I called back to him, "we are discussing your jealousy problem extensively tomorrow."

I flashed a smirk at him before stepping out into the hallway. I tried to hide my mischievous smile as I hurried back to my rooms to meet Joyriak.

"About time." She snorted as I entered.

"Sorry, I got carried away with Keylan." I beamed.

"I think I liked it better when you were hiding this thing from me." She jested.

My chalis set lunch on the table and I thanked them before sitting down with Joyriak. They bowed before exiting, leaving Joyriak and I alone to talk privately about the upcoming trip.

"So, what did lover boy pack?" She questioned.

"Uh…hiking clothes, swimsuit, lounge clothes, and he's wearing summer clothes for travel." I answered.

"What a princess." She rolled her eyes.

"Hey!" I playfully swatted her arm.

"I packed hiking clothes and a swimsuit per your request," she informed me, "I didn't pack lounge clothes, so I'll do that. And you need to stay here for a minute to pick out your travel clothes."

"Okay." I responded.

After lunch, I joined Joyriak in my closet to pick everything out.

"I think I should bring a couple other summer outfits, just to be safe." I noted, picking out some clothes.

"Don't pack too much." She warned.

"I know." I returned.

"Have you made arrangement with your halcyns and sphoas yet?" She questioned.

"Not yet…I'll go do that now." I returned.

I called my sphoas, chalis, and halcyns to inform them of what would be going on. Keylan and I had decided it would be better if I spent the night in Asphoamist and then left the next morning. I would ready myself and do my morning ritual alone. My staff, excluding Joyriak, would think I was simply spending a couple hours in my room, then waking before everyone to meet Keylan elsewhere.

Once everything was settled, I returned to Joyriak. Her brow was furrowed as she tried to fit all of my things in a bag slightly larger than the one I had taken on the last trip.

"Are you two spending the night there?" She asked.

"No, we thought it would make people too suspicious." I told her.

"Like they're not already going to be." She snorted.

"Are they?" My head snapped towards her.

"Not that I've heard." She shrugged.

"You will tell me if you hear anything, right?" I questioned.

"Of course." She replied, finally zipping my bag.

"Hey, I've been meaning to ask you," I said, "do you think it's bad that Keylan doesn't want me talking to other guys?"

"What do you mean?" She queried.

"He basically told me to stay away from the General and the Lieutenant...and Lorne." I admitted.

"Honestly, that doesn't really sound healthy." She answered.

"That's what I thought." I returned.

"You should talk to him about it...he's kind of...I don't know...odd?" She told me, "Maybe he has a good reason but he doesn't know how to express it?"

"Maybe," I sighed, "well, I have to go to Commander Jealousy now before he storms in and kidnaps me again."

"Have fun!" She snorted, handing me my bag, which was much heavier than I thought.

"Thanks, I'll call you on Wednesday to tell you all about it!" I called back to her as I exited my rooms.

I stumbled down to Keylan's rooms as I struggled with the bag I had refused to let my guards carry. I knew the officers were probably laughing underneath their helmets, but I was much too determined to carry the bag myself. I tripped into Keylan's rooms, nearly falling on my face.

"Aza? Is that you?" He called from the bathroom.

"You're lucky it is," I panted, "if it was Hanew or something everyone would know about us."

He smiled at me as he strolled out of the bathroom, only a black towel wrapped around his waist. He dried his hair with another, smaller, dark towel. My bag fell from my hands onto the floor with a soft clunk.

"Big bag." He noted.

"I've got to be prepared." I shrugged.

He chuckled as he retreated back into the bathroom to get dressed. I plopped down on the bed, staring up at the dark ceiling above me.

"So, what all are we doing tomorrow?" I questioned as he rejoined me in the bedroom.

"A bit of hiking and swimming…but it's mostly up to you." He replied.

"Could we have a picnic?" I asked cheerfully.

"If you want…I'll tell the officers to bring stuff." He beamed.

I nodded happily, excited to have this outing with my boyfriend.

"Are you going to listen to me when I teach you about the local flowers this time?" He queried as he tapped on his holopad.

"If you don't piss me off this time." I smirked.

"Hey, you know I didn't mean that." He returned.

"I'm still not sure about that." I muttered.

Keylan placed his holopad down on the bedside table as he finished tapping out orders to the officers.

"Hey." He cooed.

I ignored him as I began to tap on my own holopad.

"I told you why I had to say that stuff." He scooped me up in his arms.

"I'm just…I don't know that I'm convinced of your explanation." I confessed.

"And you decided not to mention this earlier because…?" He pressed.

"I don't know," I shrugged, "I didn't think about it until now."

"What makes you think that I don't love you? That I would ever use you for my own personal gain?" He interrogated.

"I don't think that…I don't," I replied, "I just…I don't really understand what's going on with you and the Supreme Order…especially not lately."

"I'll be able to tell you soon." He assured me.

"Okay." I beamed.

"We should go to sleep now…we'll be getting up really early." He told me.

"Okay." I chirped, slipping underneath the warm covers.

"I love you, goodnight." He whispered.

"Goodnight…love you." I mumbled in response.

When Keylan woke me the next morning, I did not bother to look at what time it was. All I knew that it was much earlier than when I normally woke up, since it was still dark outside.

"Are there any chalis or halcyns outside?" Keylan questioned an officer as I finished my morning prayers, readings, and meditations.

"No, sir." The officer replied.

"Good, have these bags taken to my ship." He commanded.

I yawned as I tried to keep my heavy lids open. Even though I'd gone to bed early, I was certainly not ready to wake up yet. As I yawned again, I felt Keylan's arms scoop me up.

"What are you doing?" I groaned sleepily.

"Go back to sleep, I'll put you on the bed in the cabin on the ship." He whispered.

"But you said we were going to have breakfast on the ship." I protested.

"You can eat when you wake up." He retorted.

"What about you?" I returned.

"I'll eat, don't worry." He chuckled.

I nodded and allowed my heavy lids to close. I drifted to sleep as Keylan carried me down the stone hallways to the hangar, where his ship was waiting for us. I was fast asleep before he even set me down in the ship's cabin.

When I woke up, I tried in vain to stretch out on the cabin's narrow bed. After hitting myself against the metal wall twice, I rolled out of the bed and stood up. I stumbled out to the cockpit, where Keylan was piloting the ship.

"Good morning, sleepyhead." He teased.

"Are we almost there?" I grumbled, sitting in the currently empty co-pilot's chair.

"Two more hours, little dove," he answered, "go get one of the officers to get your breakfast."

"Did you eat?" I queried.

"Yes, little lamb," he chortled, "now go eat!"

I grudgingly obeyed his command. Once I had eaten, I returned to the cockpit where an officer was sitting in the copilot's chair. Keylan, noticing me, ordered the officer to assist in the control room. As soon as the officer had bowed out, I plopped down on to the copilot's chair and tucked my legs underneath me.

"A little longer, princess." He informed me.

"I'm so excited." I grinned.

"Me too." He smiled.

The rest of the flight passed in silence as we enjoyed the sights outside the ship. Keylan expertly landed the ship on the beach and officers immediately came to gather our things and escort us outside.

"It's so beautiful." I remarked as I stepped on the beach.

"Take our things to the bungalow." Keylan ordered the officers.

All of them bowed and left, even though there were only a few bags

for them to carry. Once they were out of sight, Keylan pulled me

close to him.

"You look beautiful." He complimented.

"Thank you." I blushed.

"Did you sleep enough? We're not even leaving until 2300." He

continued.

"I did." I replied.

"I love you so much." He beamed.

He leaned down to kiss me, the soft breeze blowing my hair as our

lips touched.

"A whole day to ourselves." He sighed.

"I'm so excited!" I giggled, gripping his shirt tightly.

"Do you want to go the bungalow?" He inquired.

I nodded cheerfully and allowed him to take my hand. We treaded

over the soft sand to a dirt path which led through the island's

foliage and to a path made of wooden planks. This wooden path

soon turned into a bridge, which took us to a large, overwater

bungalow.

"This is huge!" I exclaimed.

"The officers took the hoverspeeders to the other side of the island," Keylan told me, "They'll stay there unless we call for them...which means we are completely and utterly alone for the entire day."

"What shall we do first?" I chirped.

"I thought we'd take a hike and maybe swim until lunch?" He suggested.

"Perfect." I grinned.

"Did you actually bring hiking clothes this time?" He smirked.

"Yes, I made sure Joyriak packed me some." I laughed.

"All right, go change." He commanded.

I pecked him on the cheek before grabbing my things and rushing to the bathroom. I noticed that even the bathroom was huge and beautiful. Once I had finished changing into the appropriate attire for our hike, I rejoined Keylan in the living room.

"Ready to go?" He asked, a hiking pack strapped onto his back.

I nodded eagerly and we stepped outside; the weather was perfect for a vacation. It was hot and sunny, but a cool breeze kept us from being overheated. It was the epitome of paradise here.

My attitude soon changed as we traveled up a large and rather rocky hill; the sun beat down on me as I tried to keep up with Keylan. He seemed to not be troubled at all, with his long legs and military training.

As we reached the top of the hill, I collapsed onto my knees and then onto my back. My chest rose and fell quickly as I tried to catch my breath. My legs burned from the exercise as I tried to regain my composure.

"This is the end of my life now," I panted, "I have climbed this hill and now…I shall die upon it."

"Oh, hush," Keylan rolled his eyes and chuckled, "we've only been hiking for 20 minutes!"

"20 minutes?!" I sat up straight.

"Yes." He chuckled, kneeling beside me.

"I'm dead. I'm dying, I've died, I'm dead." I whined.

"Come on, just down this hill and a little piece and we'll be at the lake." He encouraged me.

I groaned as he stood and helped me to my feet.

"I just want to remind you that if I die, I will kill you." I grunted as I followed him down the steep hill.

"I'll keep that in mind." He chortled.

To my delight, Keylan was right about the lake being very close to us. As soon as we reached it, I ripped my sweat-drenched clothes off my body and dove into the clear water. I waded around in the cool liquid, thankful for a break from the hot sun.

"Are you all right now?" Keylan chuckled.

"Yes." I sighed.

"Well, at least you made it to the half-hour mark." He smirked.

"How long until lunch?" I groaned.

"A couple hours until noon," He responded, "we'll swim here for a bit and then hike back."

"I can't hike anymore, babe, I'm tired!" I complained.

"Then I'll carry you." He smiled.

"No…you're not allowed to." I pouted.

"And why not?" He wrapped his arms around my waist.

"Because then YOU will be tired." I replied.

"I've carried more weight than you in training." He said.

"I'm heavier than I look." I retorted.

"I've carried you once, I can do it again." He protested.

"Not in a hot jungle for an hour." I argued.

"Wanna bet?" He smirked, lifting me from the water and carrying me out.

"No, no, no!" I shrieked.

He put me down and laughed as I pouted up at him.

"No." I scolded.

"Hey, you were the one who didn't believe me." He shrugged.

"Okay, I believe you now." I relented.

After a while of swimming, Keylan made me get out so that we could dry off and head back to the bungalow for lunch. As soon as we were back at the bungalow, we changed and carried the picnic basket to the beach on which we had parked Keylan's ship.

"Hey, I just remembered," I said as we finished lunch, "I said I would talk to you about the jealousy problem today."

"Oh, not this again." He rolled his eyes at me.

"Keylan, it's important." I retorted.

He sighed and motioned for me to continue.

"I was talking with Joyriak," I said, "and she told me it's not a good thing that you essentially ban me from talking to everyone you're jealous of."

"I don't ban you from talking to them...I just don't like it." He argued.

I raised an eyebrow at him.

"Well, what would you like me to do about it then?" He grumbled.

"Just talk to me about it. We can figure things out." I returned.

He groaned and rolled his eyes.

"Keylan, why do you get so jealous and overprotective?! I told you I don't love anyone but you, I'm just trying to be polite," I ranted, "so why are you always trying to keep me from other men? Don't you trust me?"

"It's them I don't trust." He snapped.

"Why not?" I pressed.

He remained silent and avoided my gaze.

"Keylan, babe, please don't close up again," I pleaded, "please just tell me why."

"I don't want to ruin you." He replied.

"Ruin me?" I frowned, "what do you mean?"

He took a deep breath.

"Hanew, Lorne, Chasta, all the other guys I've tried to stop you from talking to," he sighed, "they want to take advantage of you, and it's obvious. You're young, naïve, optimistic…. I love that about you, I don't want you to change, but it makes it easier for men to get what they want from you. It'll be easier for them to make you break your vows."

"Wha-what?" I stuttered.

"I know you're not…experienced with that kind of thing so I'm trying to protect you," he continued, "you know what happened to my sisters. I'm not letting anything like that EVER happen to you. Ever."

I felt my throat tighten and I moved towards Keylan. I placed my hands on either side of his face, sitting back on my heels so I could match his height.

"No one is going to…is going to….take advantage of me," I stammered, "I won't let them."

"And neither will I." He took my hands in his.

"I appreciate you trying to protect me, Keylan, I really do," I said, "but I don't need you to."

"I know that…but I want to. And I know you want me to." He returned.

"Oh fine." I rolled my eyes and blushed, giggling.

"Speaking of protection," he stood, "I brought the laserswords so we could train today on the beach. I realized we haven't trained a lot recently and I don't want you getting soft."

I scoffed as I rose to my feet to meet him.

"I'm not getting soft." I claimed.

"Really? Then fight me, *really* fight me." He handed me a sword made of eterniglass.

"Why aren't we using actual laserswords?" I interrogated.

"If I fight you without reservation, I'll kill you in seconds." He rebutted.

"Sure." I rolled my eyes.

"You start on the offensive." He smirked.

I obeyed, running at him as swiftly as I could. I ducked under his first swing and rose to deliver my own hit. Anticipating my move, he blocked my attack. I grunted in frustration as I pressed against him. I noticed he seemed rather relaxed and was only using one hand to fight me while I was struggling even though I was using both hands.

"What happened to full force?" I groaned, nodding towards his other hand.

He smirked and took hold of the sword with his other hand. Immediately, he pushed me back onto the warm sand. He swung down at me, and I slid between his legs. His shock at my move gave me time to stumble to my feet.

"Clever." He noted.

"Aren't I?" I grinned.

He began performing more advanced moves as he advanced towards me. I clumsily yet effectively blocked each hit, which seemed to be frustrating Keylan. I tried to copy his movements but ended up failing miserably. Once I figured out that I wasn't going to be able to match his skill level, I performed the moves that he had already taught me.

Even though I held my own for several minutes, Keylan did eventually get the best of me; of course, he was my lasersword trainer, he had much more experience than me, and he happened to be much larger than I was. Keylan would probably always have an advantage over me, which was why I was glad that he was on my side.

"Gotcha." He smiled, pinning me to his body and holding the sword to the back of my neck.

"Do you?" I beamed.

I pressed my lips to him and felt him soften. As soon as he had loosened his grip enough, I slid away from him and grabbed my sword again. While he recovered, I retrieved my sword and held it against his neck.

"Huh." He snorted.

"Don't let your guard down." I winked.

"If nothing else, at least you remember one of my lessons," he chortled, "I surrender, princess."

"I did okay, didn't I?" I panted.

"Much better than anyone else has ever done when fighting me," he replied, "even the General can't fight that well."

"Really?" I squealed.

"But he doesn't have a trainer as good as you do." He smirked.

"Or it's just my natural talent." I responded.

"It probably is." He chuckled.

He took my sword from me and placed it back in the bag with his.

"Are you still training with your trainer?" He inquired.

"Yeah, I did a couple extra sessions with him since we had some days off." I answered.

"Good, you need to maintain your strength." He said.

"Why?" I frowned.

"So that you can keep fighting as well as you are." He replied.

"Well, are we done with training for the day?" I moaned.

"I guess you do deserve a break after all the hiking and swimming." He shrugged.

"Yes, I do." I smiled.

"Let's go rest in the bungalow for a bit before dinner?" He suggested.

"That sounds perfect...especially since this is supposed to be a *vacation* and not a training day." I retorted.

We trekked back to the bungalow with our picnic basket and weapons bag in tow. The sun was beginning to set over the exquisite island, giving it a soft glow. I sighed happily as I padded out onto the deck of the bungalow.

"We should come here again." I said.

"Don't you want to explore some of the other islands first?" Keylan wrapped his arms around me.

"Are they as pretty as this one?" I inquired.

"Some." He shrugged.

"I think we should visit all the islands in the world together. Just the two of us." I beamed.

"We'll try." He chortled.

"When do you think we can go to another island?" I questioned.

"Next month…we need to space them properly, so people don't get suspicious." He answered.

"You've really been thinking about this, haven't you?" I giggled.

He chuckled and pressed a kiss to my cheek.

"Wait…next month is the last month you'll be here." I realized.

"Let's not think about that." He pleaded.

"What's going to happen? To us, I mean?" I interrogated.

"We are required to leave on August 31st," he told me, "You're scheduled to test out of your first set of levels on September 1st. If you pass, you'll test out of the next 5 levels exactly one week afterwards. If you pass the second test, you will test out of your final 5 levels exactly two weeks after. Granted you pass all tests, you will have one week to stay home and make preparations. You will then join me on the Supreme Order base on October 1st as an intern."

"So, we'll only be apart one month…if I pass." I clarified.

"You will pass." He returned.

"We hope." I replied.

"We know." He argued.

"But what if I don't pass?" I pressed.

"In the unlikely event that you do not pass," he responded, "I will find a way to get us together. I will come back to Asphoamist, or I will bring you to the Supreme Order base."

"When can we tell people about us?" I queried, "I know my family is going to be….weird about it…but they'll get past it."

"Or they'll kill me." He jested.

"No, they won't." I laughed.

He chuckled for a few moments before resuming his somber air.

"Leader Syphex will kill you, though," he informed me, "and Armande will try to split us up."

"Why?" I pressed.

"Leader Syphex has been so odd lately…he's completely changed. He's almost psychotic." He explained.

"And the General?" I continued.

"He's just a jealous baby." Keyan laughed.

I laughed at his accurate description of Hanew; the General did seem to be on the spoiled brat side, even though he was very kind and professional with us. I knew he'd gotten his start solely because of his high-ranking parents, even though he'd moved up so quickly only due to his skill.

"Do you want to watch holoprograms?" I asked, tired of thinking about the Supreme Order Dignitaries.

"Sure." He grinned.

We made our way into the bungalow's luxurious living room and settled into the plush couches. Snuggling together and enjoying each other's company, we watched holoprograms until the sun set.

"Hungry?" Keylan inquired as our second holoprogram ended.

"Yep." I replied.

"Okay, I'm going to make dinner." He rose from the couch.

"You're making dinner?" I raised an eyebrow at him.

"Yes." He responded.

"You know how to cook?" I laughed.

"Azalyn, I've been single and living on my own for nearly 20 years," He said, "of course I know how to cook."

"But you have people to cook for you all the time." I argued.

"I didn't always." He retorted.

"All right, impress me." I smirked.

"I will." He smiled.

I waited patiently in the living room, watching the next holoprogram that was playing on the holoprojector. The smells of the meal Keylan was cooking came wafting into the room, making my stomach grumble in response. To my surprise, it actually smelled good. I had my doubts about the Commander's cooking, but he was certainly beginning to impress me.

I floated into the kitchen, surveying the area. He had made a bit of a mess in the luxurious kitchen, but he seemed to be doing very well. I really hadn't expected the Commander of the Supreme Order to be able to cook decently.

"It smells good." I noted.

"And it meets all of your dietary needs." He beamed proudly.

"How do you know about my food allergies?" I inquired.

It was as if he had read my mind. My next question was going to be what it was and what was in it, to see if it met my dietary needs. I never had to worry about it at home since the chefs knew all my allergies, but I didn't expect him to know anything about it since I never mentioned it.

"I asked the chefs last night after dinner." He shrugged.

"I'm surprised you even thought to ask." I chuckled.

"Set the table for me?" He asked.

I nodded and went about searching the kitchen for the plates and proper utensils.

"Who's going to clean up all this after we leave?" I inquired as I set the table.

"I'll send some officers over." He replied.

"Won't someone find out?" I asked.

"I doubt Leader Syphex will even notice or care." He responded.

"Oh." I returned.

Keylan set the food onto our plates, and I smiled happily at him; he seemed to have done a nice job. We sat together at the wooden table and joined hands in prayer. We usually didn't join hands in prayer at our formal meals at home, but we were alone now, so we could. It felt rather intimate, to be praying together over dinner.

After our prayer, I hesitantly took a bite of the dinner he'd made me. He watched me intently as he ate his own food; I found myself pleasantly surprised by the food. I smiled to show him that I liked it and saw him grin in response.

Following dinner, we relaxed on a comfy bed in one of the bungalow's many bedrooms. This particular room was on the first floor and had a glass bottom which allowed us to see the tropical fish swimming underneath. We laid on our stomachs, our heads hanging over the edge of the bed so we could observe them.

We talked about the fish and the things we had seen today on our hike. We avoided heavy topics such as politics, which I liked very much. Keylan inquired after Joyriak quite a bit, making sure she was completely trustworthy. When he was satisfied with my report of her, we decided we should take a quick nap. We were both exhausted after a day of swimming, hiking, and training on the warm island.

"What time is it?" I asked Keylan as we woke up together.

"Nearly time to go." He groaned.

"We have to pack up?" I moaned.

"Yep." He sighed.

"We will go on another trip as soon as possible, right?" I whined as we packed up.

"Yes, little dove." He kissed the top of my head.

"Maybe next time we should stay longer," I suggested "it feels like we've only been here minutes."

"We stayed nearly 24 hours." He returned.

"I know," I grumbled, "but it still feels too short."

"I agree." He sighed.

"Maybe we should live here." I giggled.

"I wish." He chuckled.

Just as we finished packing up, an officer knocked on the door of the bungalow to collect our bags. We exited the bungalow together, hand-in-hand, and walked slowly along the beach to Keylan's ship.

"I didn't even get to explore the entire bungalow." I complained.

"Don't worry…it's yours now anyways." He replied.

"What?" I frowned.

"You know how I told you it's highly likely that your kingdom will be making an alliance with Waskaura soon?" He asked.

"Yeah." I responded.

"Leader Syphex has recently become very interested in making an alliance with your kingdom," he told me, "I messaged him privately a couple days ago to ask him if I could give you, the future Lumina, island 37 as a gift of good will to convince your kingdom to make an alliance with us."

"Why didn't you tell me before?" I stopped, my feet sinking into the sand.

"He didn't respond to me…until about an hour ago," he explained, "I woke up during our nap to a message from him saying that he approved it."

"So as of an hour ago, I own this island?!" I exclaimed.

"Partially." He answered.

"Partially?" I echoed.

"Leader Syphex said that since I suggested it, I would have to co-own it with you," he said, "just to make sure that you took care of everything properly. He essentially wants me responsible for anything you do... or don't do to the island."

"He doesn't trust me?" I furrowed my brows.

"He doesn't really know you, Aza." He laughed.

"True." I shrugged.

"But this island is ours now, we can come back whenever we want after the alliance is official." He smiled.

We continued on our walk to his ship, our hands swinging gently between us.

"So, you think we will form an alliance soon?" I beamed, "Between my kingdom and the Supreme Order?"

"After what Leader Syphex did for you? I think it's probable." He grinned.

"Oh, Keylan!" I hugged him tightly, "we'll finally be able to stop hiding!"

"We must wait until it's completely finalized." He warned.

"I know…but that shouldn't take more than a month," I said, "and if we make it within the week, you could be finished before summer is over!"

"Let's just worry about getting home safely right now, my princess." He smiled.

I let go of him and grinned happily up at him. He took my face in my hands and kissed my forehead before offering me a soft smile. As the officers walked up the ramp behind us, Keylan pulled me into the cockpit where he took his seat in the pilot's chair.

"Will you teach me to fly this one day?" I queried as I sat in the co-pilot's chair, "it's so different from our ships in Asphoamist."

"One day, I will, but not while we're flying for several hours." He chuckled.

"Okay." I giggled.

The trip home was a beautiful blur. I kept Keylan company for the entirety of the flight, even though I felt rather tired. We talked cheerfully about what would happen once the alliance was official, and how happy we would be. I wanted to talk about possible wedding plans, even though I knew it was much too early for that, but I decided it might frighten him. So, I stuck to lighthearted topics and continued to feel giddy the entire ride home.

As soon as we arrived back at my castle, Keylan ordered his officers away, telling them to retrieve our baggage and clean the ship later in the morning. I noticed that it was incredibly early in the morning and several hours past my usual bedtime. It seemed it was past Keylan's normal bedtime as well, as he yawned the entire walk back to his rooms.

Without dressing for bed or doing anything else, the two of us collapsed on his bed and fell asleep immediately. When I woke up the next morning, Keylan was gone.

Chapter Twenty-Four: The Decisions

I looked around, looking and listening for any sign of Keylan. After a full minute of searching for him, I realized he was definitely not in his rooms with me. I looked over at the clock, thinking perhaps he had gone to breakfast without me to let me sleep a bit longer. Seeing that it was only 7:30, I realized that he must have left for another reason. I considered calling him but thought better of it since he might be with someone else. But, who else would he be with? And why would he leave without telling me? Had something happened? Had we been caught? Had my family taken him? Had someone else taken him?

Anxious thoughts flooded my mind as I pushed off the bed. The silk sheets tangled around me, causing me to stumble as I stepped away from the bed. I threw them off in frustration, beginning to panic; I heard the main doors slide open and I froze. What if the people who took Keylan were back to take me? Who else had they taken? Who were they? What were they doing to us?

I sighed in relief as I saw that it was simply Keylan, returning in his full ensemble. He lifted the helmet off his head as I ran towards him. I wrapped my arms around his torso, pulling him to me tightly.

"Up already? You only slept a few hours." He chuckled.

"Where did you go? Why did you leave me?" I interrogated.

"I'm sorry, little dove," he apologized, "I had something to attend to."

I pulled away from him, noticing a suspiciously cheerful tone to his voice. There was no way he could be *that* happy. If I'd only slept a few hours, he'd only slept a couple; he was bound to be exhausted.

"What's going on?" I questioned.

"You'll find out soon enough, my beautiful princess." He kissed my forehead.

I giggled and blushed, enjoying this side of him. He placed his helmet on a stand near the door, momentarily leaving me. I sat on the bed as he did so, waiting for him to return his attention to me.

"When can I know?" I whined, grabbing his hands and pulling him onto the bed with me.

"Very soon, little dove." He assured me.

"Why can't you tell me now?" I pouted.

"Because it's not right of me." He responded.

"Ugh!" I exclaimed, falling back into the plush pillows.

"I'm going to have Joyriak come here this morning to get you ready," he said, "will that be okay?"

I sat up and gave him a questioning look.

"Why?" I asked.

"I want you to stay with me all morning." He grinned.

"For what reason?" I frowned.

"You'll see soon enough." He beamed.

"Are you proposing?" I queried with a joking tone.

"I'm afraid you'll have to wait a little bit longer for that." He chuckled.

"Hmm." I mused.

"Don't think too much about it," he brushed a piece of hair behind my ear, "I told you; you'll know very soon."

My mind swam with hopeful thoughts, which I tried my best to keep in check.

"You're so beautiful…I don't tell you that enough." He said.

"You don't have to…I know." I flipped my hair jokingly.

"Good." He chuckled.

We spent the next hour conversing cheerfully about our recent trip. Keylan continued to dote on me, still not giving me any clues as to what was going on. At the end of our solitary hour, Joyriak interrupted to help me get ready for the day.

"Goodness, his body's better than Lorne's." Joyriak noted as we finished our morning ritual.

"Hey, I have dibs." I hit her playfully.

"I'm just saying." She held her hands up in mock surrender.

I followed her gaze to see Keylan standing in his closet collecting his clothes for the day. A dark towel was wrapped around his waist and his dark hair glistened in the light.

"So, I guess we're skipping the bath this morning." She noted as Keylan returned to the bathroom.

"I'll just go shower after he's done." I shrugged.

"You'd better hurry." She returned.

"Babe!" I shouted.

"Yeah?" Keylan yelled back.

"Are you almost done in there? I need to shower!" I called.

He opened the door and stepped out in dark pants and a grumpy expression.

"Go." He grumbled.

"Okay, grumpy." I jested.

He stopped me with his arm as I made my way into the bathroom. He then placed a kiss onto my lips and allowed me to continue on my way. I had quite a few issues getting the shower to work, but I eventually figured it out. I borrowed Keylan's products and was out well before I needed to be.

I stepped out in the dress Joyriak had brought for me and joined my boyfriend and best friend in the living room. I sat on the floor while Joyriak fixed my hair for the day. Meanwhile, Keylan answered messages on his holopad. Glee filled me as I watched him diligently working.

"You ready to go?" He asked as Joyriak finished my hair.

I looked to Joyriak, who nodded in approval.

"Yep!" I chirped.

Keylan held his hand out to me, and I happily took it.

"I'll see you later?" I turned to Joyriak.

"Call me." She smiled

I nodded before leaving with my handsome boyfriend. We strolled down the hallway with our hands intertwined. I wondered why he was allowing us to hold hands so publicly. There didn't seem to be many people around, but we still should have been careful.

As we walked, I began to wonder what was going on. Had he told my parents about us and gotten their approval? Had he convinced my parents to let us marry to solidify an alliance between Asphoamist and the Supreme Order? What could possibly have happened that he would so publicly show affection for me?

My thoughts temporarily subsided when he dropped my hand as we approached the dining hall. We entered together to see everyone talking cheerfully. I wondered how many people already knew the news that I did not.

"Oh, good, we're all here now." My father said as we entered. Keylan and I took our seats, and I glanced over at him, trying to figure out what was going on. Miransi was seated with us, which was unusual since the Supreme Order Dignitaries and Senatorial Family were here.

"I believe most of us here do know the good news, but I thought I should formally announce it," he continued, "Asphoamist, Waskaura, and the Supreme Order have decided to form an alliance."

I smiled widely and looked over at Keylan, who looked like he was trying to hide a smile. I then looked to Lorne, who was mirroring my expression. Looking around at the others, I saw that they seemed just as happy as I was.

"We will be announcing it publicly within the week." My mother informed us.

The rest of breakfast was spent in cheerful conversation about the alliance and the ball. Lorne, Miransi, and I bombarded everyone else with questions since we were the only ones other than Lieutenant Chasta who did not know about the alliance. Not much was revealed to us, so I resolved to talk with Keylan later.

I spent the morning with my family before lunching with them in Miransi's sitting room. After lunch, we all split to rest. I decided to head to Keylan's rooms so I could find out everything about our alliance. I was insanely curious, and I also wanted to celebrate privately with him.

Keylan met me with a tight embrace as I walked into his rooms. I giggled happily as he picked me up and spun me around, making me feel more like an actual princess than I had ever felt before. He peppered me with kisses, grinning as he did so.

"What happened?" I interrogated as he finally stopped kissing me.

"Leader Syphex received intel from one of the officers that the alliance between Asphoamist and Waskaura was going to be formed this morning," he told me, "He decided that he wanted us to ally with you before they did and contacted me early this morning to call a meeting with your parents. I arranged for the meeting as early as possible then contacted Armande and Plutan about it. It was very rushed, but we formed the alliance before the Senator and Senatress even had a chance to talk to your parents."

"That's why you were gone this morning." I chuckled.

"I wanted to tell you, but I thought it would be better to let your parents do it, so you seemed genuinely surprised." He said.

"That was probably a good idea." I agreed.

"So, what shall we do to celebrate?" He wrapped his arms around my waist.

"I think I should reserve the arena and you should let me fight with a prettier lasersword." I smiled up at him.

"And I think you need more practice with the lasersword I gave you." He retorted.

"Fine." I pouted.

"But I will fight you in the arena if you can reserve it." He continued.

"I'll message Joyriak right now to set it up for us." I beamed.

I messaged Joyriak as I said I would, while Keylan went to change and gather the laserswords. When he returned, I informed him that she had everything set up for us. Thankfully, no one was even planning to use the arena for the day, so it wasn't difficult to make sure it was clear.

We met Joyriak in the desolate arena and she gave me clothes to change into. She and I excused ourselves as Keylan set everything up for our mock-fight. When I was dressed and prepared, Joyriak took her leave, wishing me luck.

"I want you to show me what you did on the beach." I said, twirling my lasersword.

"Are you sure you're ready?" He inquired.

"I don't really have a choice, babe, you're leaving me soon." I laughed.

"We're still staying until the end of the month," Keylan returned, "and besides, you'll be with me a month later."

"Possibly." I retorted.

"Definitely." He argued.

"Would you just show me the moves?" I chuckled and rolled my eyes.

Keylan smirked and began to show me the more advanced moves he had used during our mock-fight on the beach. Once I had gotten the basics of them down, we began our competition. I clumsily tried to replicate the moves he had taught me while still blocking his attacks. I fought him for longer than I had the day before, but he still knocked me back onto the dirt floor.

"Aren't you going to kiss me to distract me?" He quipped as he helped me to my feet.

"Do you want me to?" I raised an eyebrow at him.

He grinned and shrugged. I let go of his hand and threw my lasersword to the ground before tackling him with a kiss. I pinned him to the ground as he chuckled at me trying to keep him still.

"So, tell me more about the Supreme Order base." I demanded as I sat on his torso in an attempt to keep him on the ground.

"It's freezing and it's very secure." He answered.

"That's all you're going to tell me?" I scoffed.

"Everything inside is silver and red and black," he shrugged, "It's very boring."

"What is your room like?" I interrogated.

"It's large and cold and silver, like everything else on the ship," he told me, "All the furniture is black, so it's not nearly as interesting as my rooms here."

"Will I stay with you in your rooms on the base?" I pressed.

An odd expression appeared on his face.

"What is it?" I frowned.

He pushed himself up off the dirt floor of the floor, keeping my legs wrapped around him as he folded his legs.

"I've been meaning to talk to you about that, actually," he sighed, "I was going to talk to you about it yesterday, but we were having so much fun."

My heart began to beat quickly as I waited for him to continue. Would we be completely separated the entire time I lived on the base? Was he going to have to break up with me now that the alliance was made, and he was moving back to the Supreme Order base?

"I was thinking…if you're all right with it…." He stammered. My throat tightened as I waited for what seemed to be very bad news. He looked down, avoiding my gaze.

"I was thinking that maybe we could….get married? Shortly after you arrive?" He stumbled, "that way we could stay in the same room without raising suspicion?"

I was so shocked that I didn't answer. I had joked about us getting married, but I didn't think it would be happening this soon.

"I'm not proposing or anything!" He exclaimed as I continued to stay silent, "it's just…they probably won't let us be together in my rooms if we're not engaged or married. But if you're not up for it, I'll figure something out."

"So, this isn't a proposal?" I clarified.

"No…it's…it's stupid, I'm sorry. Just forget I said anything." He turned red.

"So, this is like a proposal to be engaged to be engaged?" I continued.

"Yeah...I guess." He looked back up at me.

"Well, I accept your proposal to be engaged to be engaged." I smiled.

He grinned and embraced me tightly.

"I'll give you a real proposal when I think the time is right," he whispered into my shoulder, "I don't want to rush you."

"I'm ready whenever you are." I giggled.

"I'll try to make it a surprise for you on the base." He beamed, pulling away from me.

"And you better pick out the prettiest ring." I commanded.

"The most beautiful ring for the most beautiful girl." He nodded.

"Um, Aza?" Joyriak entered the arena.

I turned to see my friend and crawled off Keylan's lap.

"Hey, what's up?" I said, dusting myself off.

"You need to get ready for dinner." She stated dryly, looking between Keylan and me.

"Okay, I'm coming." I replied.

I pecked Keylan on the lips before hurrying off with Joyriak.

"What were you two talking about?" She interrogated as we walked down the hallways.

"We kind of...we got, like, engaged to be engaged." I stuttered.

"What?!" she exclaimed, causing some patrolling halcyns to look at us.

"Hush!" I scolded.

"What does that even mean?" She whispered angrily.

"We agreed that we would get engaged shortly after I arrive on the Supreme Order base in October." I explained.

"You're going to the base? Why don't I know about this?" She questioned.

"It's not certain...I'm not supposed to be telling anyone," I told her, "I'm going to try to test out of all the levels in September. If I pass, Leader Syphex is going to allow me to intern at the base with the dignitaries."

"So, you and the Commander will get engaged then?" She clarified.

"Yep." I nodded.

"And when people ask why you're doing it so soon, what will you say?" She queried as we entered my rooms.

"Probably that we talked a bit while he was here and we developed feelings for each other," I shrugged, "and that when I came to the base, we decided to pursue a romantic relationship."

"That's still really quick, regardless." She huffed.

"I'm not going to marry anyone else, Joyriak." I informed her.

She stopped in her tracks, holding my dinner dress in her hands.

"You're young, Aza. You don't know that yet." She argued.

"Even if he leaves me and breaks my heart, I will never love another man." I asserted.

She studied my face, especially my eyes, for a full minute.

"This is insane," she sighed, "This is like those stupid fairytales from

"What do you mean?" I asked.

"You two fell in love at first sight and now you're going to get engaged just five months after meeting." She said.

"We technically met over 10 years ago." I retorted.

"If you two were dating back then, that would make him an absolute creep." She returned.

"Oh, you know we weren't!" I exclaimed, "but we have still technically known each other for years. We just happened to develop a romantic relationship over a couple months."

"You two have some type of real-life true love that I have never seen before," she put her hands on my shoulders, "and it took less than 2 months for you to develop a committed relationship. Not a healthy one for sure, but the healthiest the two of you could probably have with everything you both have gone through. That's insane."

"It's incredible." I grinned.

"I'm happy for you, I am." She sighed, "but *please* be careful."

"I'm being careful." I nodded.

She smiled and hugged me tightly before hurrying me off to dinner. I entered the dining hall to see a table full of smiling faces. Seeing everyone so happy lifted my mood as I floated over to the table.

"So, Aza, how did you celebrate the alliance?" Lorne queried as I took my seat next to him.

"Oh, uh, I just spent time with a friend." I stammered.

I glanced briefly up at Keylan, who happened to look at me at the same time. He gave me a tiny smirk before focusing on the food the chalis were setting before him.

Lorne looked between the two of us, his brows furrowing slightly. I tried to compose myself as Lorne studied my face.

"Now that everyone is informed about the alliance," my father spoke

up, "I'd like to inform everyone that the alliance between

Asphoamist and the Supreme Order will be announced tomorrow.

We will inform every one of the alliance between Asphoamist and

Waskaura on Sunday morning."

"We will announce our alliance with the Supreme Order the

following Monday." Senator Varros added.

"Why are we doing them separately?" I whispered to Lorne.

"Doing them in order of when they were formed, I guess." He

shrugged.

I nodded in agreement and turned my focus back to my food. I

wasn't going to waste my time thinking about little things like that

today; everything was going much too well.

As soon as dinner was finished, I changed and hurried off to

Keylan's rooms to continue our celebration. Joyriak promised to

cover for me if Lorne came poking around, which I assumed he

would at some point. His curiosity at how I'd celebrated, mixed with

his suspicious demeanor towards Keylan and me, was too much to

ignore.

"Do you know why we're announcing the alliances separately?" I inquired.

"No, your parents didn't discuss that with us." Keylan replied.

"Huh." I returned.

I wondered why my parents had decided to announce the alliances separately. Perhaps it was out of respect for the Supreme Order? But, if that was the case, why did Senator and Senatress Varros decide to announce their alliance with the Supreme Order next week? Were they *really* trying to do everything in order?

Keylan distracted me from these thoughts for the remainder of the night, only for them to return the next morning as we stood on the balcony. My parents had ushered my sister and I, as well as the Supreme Dignitaries, out onto the balcony that overlooked the front courtyard. Gathered below us were hundreds of people from the Asphoamist Kingdom.

"My good people of Asphoamist, we have wonderful news!" My father's voice boomed.

A hush fell over the crowd and my father turned back to my mother with a smile. They joined hands as they looked to their people.

"The kingdom of Asphoamist will be officially allying with the Supreme Order!" My mother announced.

A loud cheer arose from the crowd gathered below us. I couldn't help but smile at their happiness.

"We will no longer be under the complete power of the Supreme Order," my father explained, "but we will share our resources and aid in a mutually beneficial relationship."

My father turned back to Keylan, who stepped forward. He kept his helmet on, masking his face from the people below us.

"People of Asphoamist, the Leader is very impressed with this kingdom," Keylan said, "Asphoamist has thrived since the creation of Soturna, and I am sure this alliance will bring good fortune to both the Supreme Order and the Asphoamist Kingdom."

The cheering below us became louder and I watched happily as everyone celebrated. People were hugging, kissing, and jumping about. We had all been so worried with the recent assassinations, but now we knew our kingdom was much stronger. Keylan had informed me that we would even have a military force from the Supreme Order in our kingdom.

After the announcement, I made my way to Keylan's rooms to talk more with him about the alliance. He seemed just as ecstatic about the alliance as I was, but I still sensed that he was hiding something. Deciding that I was not going to ruin this happy day, I ignored my bad feeling.

Since the announcement, Keylan had been much more relaxed with how he acted around me in public. We walked together to dinner, his hand brushing against mine every so often. I wondered if he would decide to publicly announce our relationship now that the alliance was official.

"Perhaps we should have a ball, to celebrate the alliances." Lorne piped up at dinner.

"I don't know if we'd be able to throw together a full ball," my mother replied, "with all the preparations for the public and televised announcements… but we'll see what we can do."

Lorne looked over at me and smiled. I returned his smile, then glanced at Keylan. His helmet was off, and he was staring lovingly at me. Despite his obvious emotion, no one at the table seemed to notice…not even Hanew.

After letting Lorne escort me back to my rooms and changing for the night, I hurried off to Keylan's rooms. My heart started to beat quickly as I rushed to him, anxious to talk about our future together. Even though our time together had been brief, I had thought about our future quite a bit. Now it seemed to be all the clearer.

"Hello, my beautiful princess." Keylan greeted me with a smile.

"Hello, my handsome Commander." I responded.

I sat next to him on the couch, and we snuggled together comfortably. The holoprojector showed news announcers talking about how my parents and the Supreme Order Dignitaries would be giving an interview tomorrow afternoon about the recently announced alliance. I sighed, thinking of all the media attention we'd likely be dealing with in the coming weeks. I wondered if Keylan would be ripped from me as he fulfilled his duties to the media.

Despite the recent changes, our night and morning went as normal, which I was grateful for. Although I liked Keylan's extra attention and affection, I had grown accustomed to our normal routine. Deviating from the routine made me feel rather uneasy, especially with all that was going on in the castle.

"I'd like to inform you all that we have decided to throw a brief ball tomorrow night," my mother announced at breakfast, "we will not be able to throw a full ball with the short notice and other preparations, but we will be able to have a shortened version of our traditional ball."

"We will neglect our political duties for today and tomorrow in order to prepare for the ball." My father added.

Everyone smiled happily at the news. The previous balls were a welcome break from political meetings and duties, and this one would be no different.

"Aza, did you want to choreograph some dances for the ball?" Lorne asked as he pulled me aside after breakfast.

"Um, sure," I stammered, "but only until lunch. I'll need to go get ready for tomorrow with my alysseas then."

"Okay." He grinned.

He took my hand and practically dragged me to the dance studio, not allowing me to glance back at Keylan. Once there, I changed into appropriate clothes and joined him on the dance floor. We choreographed dances until lunch, and I found myself incredibly thankful for a break.

After a lunch with my family, planning with my alysseas, and dinner, I got ready for bed and snuck off to Keylan's rooms. I hoped that his excitement about the recent alliance would mitigate any jealousy he felt. When he embraced me with a smile, I realized that my hopes were met.

"Are you excited for tomorrow?" He inquired sweetly.

"Yes, are you?" I returned.

"Of course," he beamed, "have you decided what you're going to wear?"

"A red dress. Daska picked it out." I told him.

"I'm so excited to see you in it." He grinned.

"What? Are you just excited to see me in a ball gown?" I teased.

"You look so beautiful in the ballgowns you wear." He responded.

"Do I not look beautiful in other clothes?" I challenged.

"You know you do." He chortled.

We spent the night together once more, only for me to be hurried back to my rooms the next morning by Joyriak so I could prepare for the ball. The ball was going to start earlier than usual, even though it was only going to last four hours instead of six; my parents wanted everyone to be well rested for the coming media and official engagements.

My alysseas and I spent our day trying our best to adequately prepare for the ball. I didn't feel as prepared as I usually did, but I still felt confident that I looked beautiful. This time, we entered the ball together, since it was a less formal affair. I quickly separated from them to join my family, who were chatting cheerfully with some of the noble families of Asphoamist.

Beside us, couples whirled around on the dance floor. I watched with great interest as Keylan danced with Captain Plutan. They seemed to be in the midst of an intense discussion, their voices lowered so I could not hear them as they spun by.

"Ah, Azalyn, you're finally here." My mother noted as I joined them.

"I'm sorry, we all took a bit longer to get ready." I replied.

"You look beautiful, would you like to dance?" Lorne asked as he pushed into our group.

"Of course, Lorne." I smiled politely.

For the entirety of the formal hour, I was exchanged between Keylan, Hanew, Lorne, Chasta, and occasionally Plutan. I had planned to catch my breath at some point but realized when Ithan announced l'heure des amis that this plan was not going to work for me.

"We have to do the dances we choreographed yesterday!" Lorne exclaimed.

I nodded and smiled, trying to hide how out of breath I was. Though I felt exhausted from being spun around my several people, I managed to perform my dances with Lorne well and stay on my feet for the rest of the hour. Thankfully, Joyriak was there to keep Lorne occupied for most of the dances.

As soon as the social hour began, I shuffled over to the refreshments table. I had been kept so busy by my friends and the guests that I had not had a single sip of water in the hour and a half that I had been here. Unfortunately for me, my break did not last long as I was whisked off by my parents to converse with various political figures.

269

When the partner only hour began, I felt both relieved and fearful. This would be the last hour of the night, but I could tell by the way that Keylan, Lorne, and Hanew were looking at me that I would not get a rest for the next hour. I tried to be gracious and polite as each of them swung me about the floor. Just as he had apparently planned, Keylan got the last dance of the ball with me.

"Are you okay?" He questioned.

I realized he was the first to pose that question; either no one had noticed how tired I was, or they had not had the chance to ask me.

"Tired." I simply replied.

"We'll go straight to my rooms after the ball," he returned, "I'll help you with your gown and hair."

"Okay." I nodded.

As he had promised, Keylan led me straight to his rooms as soon as the ball was officially over and helped me undress for bed. I snuggled into his bed as I waited for him to join me and give me his warmth. When he finally joined me, I cuddled into him and fell asleep quickly.

Chapter Twenty-Five: The Conflict of Interest

I woke up later than I normally would on a Sunday, knowing that we would be attending the church's evening service in place of the morning service as a result of last night's ball. As I blinked awake, I saw Keylan stopped in the middle of the floor between the bathroom and the bed. He was frowning down at his holopad, as if he were confused.

"What's going on?" I groaned, sitting up in bed.

"Your parents have summoned us for an announcement." He answered.

I furrowed my brows and looked at my holowatch. I too had a message from my parents, summoning me to meet them on the main balcony for a very important announcement. There were no details listed, only a time for me to be there.

"9:30?!" I exclaimed, "I need to get going...why didn't you wake me earlier?

He frowned and padded back over to me. He checked his holopad.

"Mine says 10:00." He replied.

"Why do I need to be there early?" I frowned.

He shrugged and walked back over to his closet.

"Do you know what this is about?" I pressed, "I don't have any details."

"It's probably something about the alliance." He answered.

"Boring." I laughed.

I stood and fixed my hair quickly before pulling my dress on.

"I'd better get going, I'll see you soon." I called out.

"Love you!" He responded, his voice muffled.

"Love you too." I whispered as I exited his rooms.

Once I was ready for the apparently very important announcement, I hurried off to the balcony. Somehow, I made it there five minutes early and saw Lorne waiting alone.

"Hey, what's going on?" I asked, looking around for others.

"No idea," he shrugged, "my parents just told me to be by the balcony at 9:30."

"So why are you here at 9:25?" I raised an eyebrow playfully.

"Why are *you* here at 9:25?" He repeated with the same playful tone.

"Touché." I giggled.

We looked out the glass doors to see a crowd gathering below us. The courtyard was bathed in beautiful sunlight. I was glad that we had good weather today, as it appeared we might be outside for a while.

"It's a beautiful morning." He commented after a few minutes of silence.

"It is." I agreed.

We stood there in peaceful silence for a few moments more. Though I wanted to be snuggled up in bed with Keylan and not standing by the balcony doors, I appreciated the scenery. It reminded me a bit of the day Keylan and I had spent on the Supreme Order's private island.

"Listen, Aza," Lorne sighed, "I have something to tell you."

"Yeah?" I turned towards him.

He furrowed his brows and bit his lip. He groaned and turned away from me, as if he were unable to say what he was thinking.

"You look beautiful this morning." He stuttered, staring out the window.

"Is that it?" I chuckled, "I mean, thank you, but…"

"No…. I just don't know how to…" he mumbled.

He turned back to face me and took a deep breath. I giggled nervously and raised an eyebrow at him, as if to ask him why he was acting so weird. I thought perhaps he knew why we were gathered here this morning.

Lorne moved closer to me, making me nervous. He stared intently at me, his eyes drifting back and forth between my eyes and my lips. I folded my arms over my chest protectively.

"What are you doing?" I chuckled, "is there something on my face or…. or something?"

In one graceful movement, Lorne cupped my face with his hands and pressed a passionate kiss to my lips. My eyes widened in shock as I pushed him away.

"What the hell was that?" I exclaimed.

"I…. I…I…" he stammered.

"Oh good, you two are already here!" My mother interrupted.

"You did say 9:30, maima," I replied, "and it's well past now."

"How are you two feeling?" She smiled.

"Fine." We shrugged in unison.

"Are you two ready to go out on the balcony?" My father inquired, joining us.

"I suppose." I sighed.

My mother stepped towards me and smoothed out my dress, then my hair. She offered me a gleeful smile before pulling me into an embrace. I gave her a questioning look as she joined hands with my father. Senator and Senatress Varros soon arrived, giving us all a polite bow of the head. Senatress Varros copied my mother's movements, smoothing out her child's hair and outfit.

"Everyone ready?" My father looked at us.

We all responded with a nod; Lorne and I wore confused expressions while the rest of them looked ecstatic. My parents waltzed out onto the balcony and waved to the citizens gathered below. Once the cheers of the crowd had died down, the Senator and Senatress followed their lead.

As soon as the applause was finished, our parents turned back to us and motioned for us to follow. Lorne tried to take my hand as our parents turned to the crowd below; I shot him a dirty look before shaking his hand off. Under usual circumstances, I would have welcomed this comforting gesture. However, he had lost his privileges as a result of his previous actions.

"My good people of Asphoamist," my father announced, "we will be making our important announcement very soon."

Everyone cheered below us once more as we waited patiently for the Supreme Order Dignitaries to arrive. Lorne and I found ourselves smooshed together as the Senator and Senatress moved over to make room for them. Keylan and Hanew entered the balcony first, greeting the crowd below with a simple lift of the hand. Plutan and Chasta followed them, acknowledging the citizens with a nod of the head.

"As many of you have likely guessed," my father's voice boomed over the crowd, "we have made an alliance with the kingdom of Waskaura. We will trade supplies as needed and help each other in times of war."

The crowd cheered enthusiastically; I smiled at how happy they were. Tensions were high from the looming threat of war, but every alliance made us stronger.

"We have been in meetings with the Senator and Senatress of Waskaura," he continued, "and we have decided to solidify this alliance with a marriage."

I frowned and looked over at Lorne. His eyes were wide, and a smile played across his lips. I scrunched my nose in confusion as I looked back at my father.

"The marriage of my daughter, Azalyn, to the Senatorial Son of Waskaura, Lorne Varros." He shouted happily.

My jaw dropped and I felt the blood drain from my face. My father motioned for us to step up to the edge of the balcony. I stayed frozen in my spot until Lorne grabbed my hand and pulled me forward. He waved gleefully to the crowd before lifting my hand up triumphantly. He then pulled me close and pressed a sloppy kiss to my lips.

I pushed him away angrily and stepped back. I shook my head in disbelief as I stared around at everyone. My parents, the Senator, and the Senatress all looked overjoyed while the General and the Lieutenant looked shocked. I looked around for Keylan anxiously and discovered that he was no longer on the balcony.

"It looks like we have a shy bride." My father chuckled.

The crowd's lighthearted chuckle was enough to make me sick. Did they really think that's why I was freaking out? Because I was shy? Could they *really* not see that I was panicking? I had just had my marriage, which I certainly did not approve of, announced to me in front of an entire kingdom!

I ran through the stone hallways, ignoring everyone who tried to speak to me. I kicked off my shoes as I ran, feeling restricted by them. Tears rolled down my cheeks and my throat began to burn as I ran straight to Keylan's rooms. To my chagrin, his officers were gone. I prayed to God that this did not mean he had left.

"Keylan?" I knocked on the door.

There was no answer, but one look at the lockpad next to the door told me he was there. I banged on the door, hoping he would answer me.

"Keylan, would you *please* open up?" I yelled, "it's me! It's Azalyn!"

I knew he knew it was me, but I couldn't help it. Why wouldn't he open the door? Why wouldn't he answer *me*?

"I promise you, I didn't know anything about any of this!" I screamed, "I'm...I'm sorry! Please just open the door! Just talk to me! Please!"

I realized as I sobbed how lucky I was that no one appeared to be anywhere near his rooms. Not that I cared whether or not anyone heard me. I didn't care about anything anymore; not if I had to marry Lorne. I sunk to my knees at this thought and leaned upon the door to his rooms for support.

I cried myself to sleep, still leaning upon the cold metal door to Keylan's rooms; my dreams were filled with panic and horror. Visions of me walking down an aisle with tears running down my face to see Lorne dominated my sleep through the respite. Despite these terrifying dreams, I did not wake.

The only time I did awaken was when I felt strong arms lifting me from the ground. I coughed a couple times, trying to clear my throat of the smoke which currently impaired my vision. After blinking awake, I peered through the smoke to see the identity of the person holding me.

"Key...Keylan?" I stuttered.

Keylan did not answer, simply looked ahead. His helmet covered his head, shielding his face from my view. Instead of focusing on him, I turned my gaze to the area surrounding us. There was a horrible stench in the air, and I wanted to know what the cause of it was. As my eyes scanned the scene, I heard a scream. The adrenaline pulsing through my veins sharpened my vision and I was able to catch a glimpse of what surrounded us. Lying on the floor were the bodies of what seemed like hundreds of people to me. I gasped in fear, unable to scream because of the dryness of my throat.

I gripped Keylan's shirt tightly, as if he were going to drop me with them. I looked back up at him and silently cursed his stupid helmet. I wanted to know what was going on and what his feelings about the situation were.

"What's going on?" I croaked.

He remained silent as he continued to carry me.

"Keylan, what's happened?!" I attempted to shout.

"He's taking the Cerulea!" One of the halcyns yelled.

I turned to see a halcyn, unidentifiable because of the smoke surrounding us, rushing towards us. Keylan's steps did not slow, nor did he falter. He just continued to walk straight ahead, to some undisclosed location. I realized as a Supreme officer intercepted the halcyn why Keylan had not seemed worried.

A few more steps in the same direction allowed me to see where we were headed. I frowned as the shape of the Supreme Order Dignitaries' ship became more and more clear. Keylan's heavy footsteps echoed in my ears as we came to the ramp of the ship.

"Babe, where are we going?" I squeezed his shirt for emphasis.

He did not say a word as he carried me to some sort of medical room and laid me on one of the beds. He peeled my arms off him as he stood above me. I watched as he retrieved his lasersword from his belt, holding it tightly in his gloved hand.

"Keylan, what are you doing?" I questioned.

"Go back to sleep, Azalyn." He commanded.

"I want to know what's going on." My voice broke.

"Put her to sleep and don't let her leave," he ordered a doctor standing in the corner of the room, "put the captain in charge of protecting her when she returns."

The doctor nodded timidly as Keylan stormed off, igniting his lasersword as he left me.

"Key-Keylan!" I yelled, trying to get off the bed.

I stumbled, suddenly feeling very dizzy.

"Sit down please, Cerulea," the doctor pleaded, "you've inhaled a lot of smoke."

She helped me back onto the bed and placed a patch on my arm.

"I want to know what's going on...I want Keylan." I told her.

"Everything will be fine soon, Cerulea." She assured me.

With that final reassuring statement, I fell into a deep sleep on a medical bed on the Supreme Order Dignitaries' ship.

To be continued in **Time: Part Three.**

www.ingramcontent.com/pod-product-compliance
Lightning Source LLC
Chambersburg PA
CBHW060303260626
47160CB00007B/2488